YOLANDA JOE

A GEORGIA BARNETT MYSTERY

SIMON & SCHUSTER

NEW YORK LONDON TORONTO SYDNEY

SIMON & SCHUSTER
Rockefeller Center
1230 Avenue of the Americas
New York, NY 10020

For information about special discounts for bulk purchases,
please contact Simon & Schuster Special Sales at
1-800-456-6798 or business@simonandschuster.com

Designed by Karolina Harris

Manufactured in the United States of America

10 9 8 7 6 5 4 3 2 1

Library of Congress Cataloging-in-Publication Data

Joe, Yolanda.
Video Cowboys : a Georgia Barnett mystery / Yolanda Joe.
p.   cm.
1. Barnett, Georgia (Fictitious character)—Fiction. 2. African American television
journalists—Fiction. 3. Women television journalists—Fiction. 4. Chicago (Ill.)—Fiction. I. Title.

PS3560.O242V53 2005
813'.54—dc22   2005042470

ISBN 0-7432-5038-9

ACKNOWLEDGMENTS

A special thanks to my top-gun agent, Victoria, for her friendship, hard work, and help throughout my career. I would also like to thank my editor, Tara, for her ideas and her wonderful enthusiasm. Ladies, both of you have been invaluable to me. This mystery novel is a better book because of you.

In loving memory of Vert Colbon. . . .
A wonderful woman who liked to read,
loved to encourage, and played a killer hand of Bid Whist.

Story Slug = Hostage Standoff
Special Report

Anchor Intro

(PETER BRADFORD READS)

CLOSE UP

We interrupt this broadcast to bring you a special report.

Channel 8 News has learned of a hostage situation at Lake Michigan Bank.

Details are sketchy but here's what we do know: there is at least one gunman and more than six hostages.

We will bring you updates on this breaking story as soon as they become available.

Channel 8's Georgia Barnett is live at the scene.

Live at the scene? Hmph, that's putting it mildly. I was actually *in the bank* when all hell broke loose. Then to top it all off—well, wait a second; let's not get ahead of ourselves. Let's deal with how I'm feeling now.

For the first time in my life I'm covering a story that's scaring the living stew out of me. Remember the song

"Respect" by Aretha Franklin? You know how serious Miss Re-Re gets when she croons *"Real-Real-Real-Real"*?

Well . . . FOR REAL. That's how serious I am.

And for those of you who don't know me, don't jump to conclusions. I'm not timid or naïve. I'm just in a bad spot—no wait, that's like calling the kettle a teapot. I'm in a sinkhole.

Oh yeah, it's that deep.

Walk in my pumps today. Wouldn't it put the fear of God in you, if how you did your job one day would determine whether or not one of your closest friends lived or died?

I'll bet you just kicked off my pumps and decided you'd rather go barefoot, huh?

That's exactly how I felt. But what choice did I have? There was absolutely no way that I could shake off the responsibility I had just been saddled with.

You see, Zeke—that's my cameraman—he and I were so happy. We'd landed an easy, early morning shift. We'd just finished covering a news conference at the United Center sports arena. An Olympic basketball player had decided to defect from China while on a visit to Chicago. It was causing an international stir. There was a ton of press on hand. But it was one of those big fat *prime-time/ face-time* stories that veteran news folks like us know how to handle with ease. Our day was *cake—or so we assumed.* That *cake* was about to be tossed upside down. And baby, there wouldn't be *nothing sweet about it.*

Like Miss Re-Re sings, *"Real-Real-Real-Real."*

Things got a little *too real* for me. Luckily I had help. Who needs the cavalry? I had a dynamite group of guys on my side known as the VIDEO COWBOYS.

1

"Yeah baby!" Zeke howled inside our cramped news truck. His howl had the volume of a moon-baying wolf on Prozac and the silliness of Scooby-Doo.

The truck pitched and swerved as Zeke changed lanes left, slammed on the brakes, then changed lanes back. I've had smoother rides on a roller coaster. Zeke acted like he was on a Six Flags ride too, the way he flung both hands in the air and then used his beer belly to hold the steering wheel straight. We had just worked the sunrise newscast.

"Hey-hey," he said in a singsong voice. "It's 9 A.M. on a Friday and we're done for the day. My wife is on a cruise with her sisters. I already called my boys and they'll be waiting for me at the bar for burgers and beer 'round noon. Hot damn. Jesus must be a cameraman."

"If he was," I said while waiting for all my vital organs to shift back into their rightful spots, "he'd drive at a normal speed. Say Zeke. Do a sister a solid and stop off at the bank."

"Amen to the bank. It's my turn to buy and it ain't gonna be cheap, Georgia. The Video Cowboys guzzle booze like Prohibition's coming back."

"Say Zeke. Who came up with that nickname any-way?" I played with the press pass around my neck from the news conference we had just covered. "It's so cool."

"Yours truly, of course." Zeke winked. "I hung that joker on 'em 'bout two years ago. They had just started freelancing after being laid off by the corporate bean counters that took over Channel 8. The Video Cowboys are throwbacks. They'll take on ANY STORY ANY TIME—day or night—no matter how tough it is."

"Which one of the Cowboys is the baddest, Zeke?"

Zeke vigorously scratched his chin. His lanky fingers grated against seven-day-old stubble. He repeated my question thoughtfully, "Who *IS* the baddest?"

"Can't be Choke," I said, throwing out my first thought. I visualized Vicente Ochoa—Choke. He's a little guy. Everything about him is compact—his 5'6" height, his cropped hair, his choppy laugh, even his 1992 Plymouth. He has beautiful, thick shiny hair and dreamy eyes. Choke is a *frequent flier flirt* too. And dancing? I went to his sixty-first birthday party last year; good God that man can jam on the dance floor. Choke can boogie like Bootsy Collins and slow dance like Smokey Robinson. "Naw, it can't be Choke."

"The Salsa King? You're right. Not him. Besides, that guy has more dance trophies than Bayer has aspirins."

That's the truth. I made up my mind right then

and there. I told Zeke I was casting my vote for Paulie.

Zeke slammed on the accelerator, blowing through a yellow light. Then, suddenly, as if he'd just heard me, he said very Soprano-like, "Paulie Vitale? My Paulie?"

"Don't go there Zeke. I'm not stereotyping just because Paulie is Italian . . ."

"And grew up in Little Italy with all the grandsons of Al Capone's crew, naw, that wouldn't make you say he's the baddest, huh?"

I smacked Zeke on the arm with my notepad. "Don't go there! It's just that Paulie is such a big guy. He's what, 230 pounds?"

"That's on a ghetto scale," Zeke laughed. "Told me he went to the doctor last week and weighed in at 265."

"Dawg, he doesn't look it. He carries it well."

"Height. He's 6'3", Georgia. But the doc says he's gotta lose fifty pounds."

"What?! Paulie's gonna have to give up all that imported tobacco he loves." I laughed. "'Cause if he loses fifty pounds and keeps smoking that pipe, somebody's bound to mistake him for a crack addict."

We finally stopped at a red light. Zeke banged out a drum roll on the dashboard and announced, "Wayne 'Gunner' Anderson is the baddest."

"Get out of here."

"Oh yeah."

"C'mon Zeke. Gunner's the biggest loner since the Unabomber. He only talks to you guys."

"And you."

"Only because we're tight."

"True, Georgia. Gunner is a solemn son of a gun around other folks besides us. He stays home every day listening to police scanners and the fire department frequency. He calls Paulie and Choke and tells them where to go to cover a breaking story. Gunner keeps all the books too. He knows what they shot and who bought the video."

"So what? He's organized. That makes him tough?"

"You know how he got the name Gunner?" Zeke asked, turning into the outdoor parking lot of the bank.

"Yeah. He used to ride in the TV choppers shooting aerials of fires and stuff for the morning show."

"Right," Zeke said, wrestling the news truck into a tight spot. "But Gunner was also in Vietnam. He rode in the choppers there too: on machine gun. He saved half a platoon once near the Thai River. Kept the enemy off until they could reestablish position and hold that key spot."

"He's a straight-up war hero?" I said, giving him serious props in his absence. "You go, boy."

"We're impressed. Think the bean counters were? HELL NO. All those suits do is count the number of heads *holding a camera.* They never take into account the heart of the man *behind the camera.* When they forced all the old camera guys out, I went up to the manager's office and told that chump he was off his rocker. Told him about Gunner and the medals he won in the war."

"Obviously that didn't help."

"In fact it hurt. Gunner never said a word about his military record to the guy. When Gunner found out that I had gone up there and told the new boss—he punched me in the chops. Sucker punched this old southern boy but good, Georgia."

"Why'd he hit you?"

"Told me he was a soldier, always was one, and always will be and a good soldier takes his marching orders without question. No excuses and no begging for reprieves. If they wanted him OUT, then he was GONE. Gunner don't play."

We got out of the truck. Zeke grabbed his equipment box. It contained spare batteries and a set of lights. Then he grabbed a sack of power cable before slinging the camera up on his shoulder. "Whatya doing? We're NOT moving into the bank for God's sake. We're just making a quick withdrawal."

"Obviously you missed the memo."

"What memo?"

"It's posted all over the station. Someone's been breaking into trucks and stealing the equipment. Two guys over at NBC got their cameras ripped off. That ain't happening to me, Georgia."

"Better not. And I can't imagine it will, the way you baby this equipment."

"Hmph. Right about now I'm wishing I had a stroller to put it all in," Zeke said as he huffed up the walkway with the massive gear.

I took one of the bags from Zeke, the lightweight one of course, and we headed inside the bank.

The line stopped me cold: ten people, and only two tellers. "Forget this, Zeke. Let's try the ATM."

"Can't," Zeke said, dumping the equipment in a pile to our left, getting it out of the way of the other customers in line. He reached into his pocket. "No cash card. I'm a passbook guy."

"Well aren't you the Fred Flintstone of finance. Why don't you have an ATM card?"

"It's too easy to take money out and too easy for

somebody to rip you off—including the bank with all those *stick 'em up* withdrawal fees."

"You got ah point there."

Two more customers were called to the counter by a pinging sound and a blinking red arrow. Zeke limped forward.

"How's the leg?" Zeke had hurt it during a friendly game of basketball between the Channel 8 guys and another television station. "Still bothering you?"

"Still gimpy. How's Doug?"

"Grouchy 'cause he's on light duty."

"Even though it landed him a free trip to Mexico?"

My boyfriend, Detective Doug Eckart, was down in Mexico waiting to bring back a retired Chicago politician who fled there after being convicted of corruption. Doug had gotten the easy assignment because he was just getting over a bum leg. He tore a ligament during a skiing trip we took together a while back and didn't even know it. Not until his doctor told him he had to have surgery, that is, and then boyfriend knew it FOR SURE. I had a thought that made me laugh.

"What's funny?" Zeke asked.

"I guess white men can't jump and black men can't ski."

We laughed together.

That gorgeous blend of sound gave me a warm feeling inside. I guess that's why I jumped so when the cold, deafening sound of a gunshot shattered the peaceful moment. Yeah . . . *real-real-real* . . . a real gunshot.

Everyone in the bank reacted differently. Some screamed. Some were quieted by fear. Half of the people froze and the other half hit the floor. Zeke and I had a twin reaction. We were both half-squatted down, heads up, our gazes raking the room for the source of the shot.

Now what do you think a gunman would look like? A gunman with the guts to come into a bank to rob the joint in broad daylight? I figured a big guy, wearing a mask. Very plain clothes. Someone carrying a large bag to stash the cash in. If he's solo in the bank, he's probably got someone waiting in a car outside with the motor running, right?

Wrong as Shaq in drag.

I wouldn't cast this guy as a bank robber no more than I'd cast Britney Spears in a remake of *The Flying Nun*.

This man was white, about 5'10", slender build, a gaunt face with prickly grayish brown growth on his cheeks and chin. He had a pronounced nose, sharp and angling to the left. His deep black eyes were very cold and determined. He wore a strange getup—a black sweatshirt with a light blue sea horse on it. His trousers were too big; the cuffs had been doubled up by hand, floating above his ashy, bare ankles and a pair of dirty white Keds sneakers. He had a bag—a red sack with a white drawstring and black lettering that said LAUNDRY. But the bag couldn't be to stash the cash in—it was already full; something was in it. But what? I asked the question in my head. What's in the bag?

"I've got a bomb!" the gunman shouted.

Sorry I asked.

"And I'm gonna use it . . ."

Don't tell me no mo'.

I felt Zeke tense beside me. I didn't even look at him. I was studying this guy with the bomb in the sack and the gun pointed at the guard who was standing by the door.

"Take the money and go," the guard said.

"Please!" one of the tellers groaned.

"Shut up!" The gunman set the bag ever so gently on the counter so everyone could see it. "Everybody just shut up and listen or we're all gonna die. Now," he pointed at the guard, "put your gun on the floor and slide it over."

The gunman looked like one of those homeless guys selling newspapers. *But don't let nobody fool you.* There was an edge to him—like at one time things were really good—and now things are really bad. I'm a TV news vet and I can size up people pretty darn well. This gunman was desperate and whatever he had in mind to do, it was going to be full speed ahead.

The guard followed directions to the vowel, child. He moved slowly, easing his gun belt onto the floor and sliding it away with a soft kick.

"Lock the door. Close the blinds too."

The guard went to the door and locked it. He yanked on the gnarled drawstring and turned day into a dusky evening. That's when I noticed something, something important.

I spotted a little boy no older than seven, fidgeting on his knees, looking around, panting, alone. What was a seven-year-old kid doing alone in a bank?

Ten feet away from us, a door began to screech open.

The gunman cast his gaze and his gun in that direction. The little boy jumped up and ran toward his pregnant mother, who was coming out of the restroom.

"Mama!"

Her smile turned into a muffled "Oh God!" as she realized what was going down.

The gunman glared at her, glanced at the little boy, then bit his lip and cast his eyes back and forth. He seemed angry that he had not cased the situation properly, and was clearly *distracted* by his error. That's when Zeke made a move. He lunged forward. *Somehow* the gunman sensed it coming and took a jerky step backward. Zeke grazed his right side, knocking his gun hand up.

Meanwhile, the guard had flipped the lock and swung the door open, yelling for people to run. Like he had to tell 'em? Please. Bank customers were running the 100-yard dash toward the door already. Chivalry is dead and buried in a shallow grave with Fear standing over it holding the shovel. ALL THOSE PEOPLE were cutting in front of the pregnant woman and her son.

The guard took a run toward his gun on the floor. *The gunman* took a SWING at Zeke, grazing his temple with the butt of the gun, opening up a small cut. Then he threw ANOTHER PUNCH that caught Zeke in the throat. *That did it.* Zeke slumped over, grabbing his neck.

I was trying to push the pregnant woman and her son out of the door ahead of me. *Too late.* A gunshot shattered the ceiling tile above our heads. I froze. The rest of the people, who were just steps from freedom as well, froze too. The guard slid to a stop, just a step or two away from his gun on the floor.

"Nobody else move! Get on your knees now!"

We dropped to our knees.

The gunman turned on Zeke and took aim. "Why don't people listen to me? You're trouble, man. Just like the rest of them. You wanna hurt me, don'tcha?"

Zeke made a choking sound.

"Don't!" I shouted. "Don't kill him."

The gunman stared at me. His stone-washed face came alive with the prickly red color of blood rushing to his head.

"Let me help him," I said, then slowly moved beside Zeke. A little bit of blood from his forehead got on my clothes. Zeke pulled a long, white hanky out of his pocket. I took it and held it against the cut on his head. Zeke just winced. He wasn't hurt too bad but defeat STINGS.

The gunman leaned forward and pushed the gun into the middle of my chest. I felt a chill roll up my spine and my mouth became desert-dry.

"TV people?" he said, tapping the laminated media pass that hung around my neck. The gunman stepped back and motioned with his pistol toward the pile of equipment.

"Okay." He appeared to perk up. "TV people. You're gonna help me."

He needed help? *You've gotta be kidding me.* He's packing a gun, toting a bomb, and sporting a deadly attitude and HE was reaching out to US *for help?* This is the kind of unpredictable drama that makes you bust out in a pool of perspiration, that makes your head hurt, your eyeballs bug out. *Oh drama.*

The simple fact that Zeke was with me helped more than a smidgen. If you're in a tight spot and don't know what the heck is going on, it's good to have someone you can trust around. Although I could kick his butt for taking a run at the guy and almost getting his head blown off in the process, Zeke did save some folks. Five people made it out safely before the gunman shot in the air. That left a total of ten people. Three customers. Two tellers. The guard. Plus the pregnant woman and her son. Zeke and, of course, me.

Do I seem like a martyr? 'Cause I'm not. I used to run track. I wasn't Flo Jo but I could fly. My mother teases me all the time about how when I was *real little* I'd take off running whenever I got scared. She loves to tell this story.

According to Mama I was a lazy toddler. My older cousins thought I was cute as pie (and seeing my baby pictures I can safely say they are right as rain) and because my great aunt was too cheap to buy them Barbie dolls, my cousins would carry me around on their hips all the time. Not my twin sister Peaches—she was too ornery to let anyone pick her up but Mama.

Anyway, they carried me around so much that I was late walking. They said Peaches stood up seven months before me and started switching with her hand on her hip. In literature, that's called *foreshadowing*. In life, that's called *fast ass*. Peaches was strutting her stuff, putting to shame every peacock in any hemisphere near or far INCLUDING the electronic NBC logo. Meanwhile I was STILL sitting on my behind in the middle of the floor.

One day a thunderstorm swept through Chicago, and if I'm lying I'm flying, wind in Chicago is *nothin'* to play with. Gusts can uproot trees, down power lines, snatch shingles off a roof the way a crook snatches a purse. This storm had a howling wind and lightning streaking across the sky; it shook the house with thunder that sounded like a cannon. The lights flickered too. Mama says I got so scared that I jumped up and started running down the hallway. Before that I hadn't even made an effort to pull up on the furniture, let alone stagger a couple of steps in my Stride Rites. I took off like I had on a pair of Nikes and my life depended on it.

Speed I had. Courage came along later. That's why I

tried to push the expectant mother and her son out the door; unfortunately, I just didn't have the time. The gunman decided that he couldn't trust ANY of us after what Zeke tried. So he started giving orders.

"Everybody get in the center of the room; sit Indian style, back to back, in a circle, quick. No yapping."

I stood up slowly, fear forming icicles on my joints, but still I was DETERMINED to help Zeke.

"Leave him alone," the gunman scolded. "He's all right."

I started to argue but I could tell he was still jumpy. Boyfriend was twitching something fierce. He was a slender man, but slight, as in he hadn't been getting enough to eat on a regular basis. My mama could fix that; she'd force-feed a stray cat a bowl of grits and half a pan of biscuits if she thought it looked scrawny. But I hoped to high heaven that he wouldn't be lucky enough to get a home-cooked meal *from nobody*. If you asked me, all he had coming was a state pen lunch—bread and bologna, hold the mayo and the metal escape file.

The gunman spit out a threat. "I'll shoot anybody that I gotta. I will."

Who was he trying to convince, himself or us? His voice was firm but not terrorizing, more reluctant and dry. He hadn't *even looked* in the direction of the tellers when he came in. His makeshift sack was conspicuous. He must've flunked Bank-Robbing 101. Or maybe he had some other wacky agenda, but what? I mean REALLY. What did he want and what was he doing here? And more importantly would he make good on his threat and kill us all?

I measured the mixed bag of people in our hostage

powwow, hoping for just one undercover S.W.A.T. team specialist. One man, white, in his thirties, had on a business suit and some expensive kicks. I love shoes. *And his were lovely.* Those bad boys were *Prada.* Boyfriend was making some bucks *whatever* he did for a living. He was average height, stocky, clean-shaven, dark hair, salon cut, and wore round specs.

The other guy couldn't be more than twenty or so, Hispanic. He had on a biking helmet, jeans with knee guards—like hockey goalies wear only smaller, and a shirt that said Super Duper Messenger Service.

The last guy was African-American, middle-aged. Had a lot of worry lines in his face, a scruffy beard, thinning hair, worn pants, old leather belt, and worn-out work shoes.

Both women were twenty-something, white, dressed in business attire fitting tellers. One was a redhead with a sassy short cut; the other had long blond hair and wore big block glasses. They were clinging to each other so I take it they were friends.

The guard may have been our best bet. He was short but had a well-built body. Big chest. You could see the muscles bulging beneath his tan uniform. His protruding jaw met you first like the knob on a closed door. He was white, completely bald, about fortyish, but very tan, like *overexposed in Cancun* tan. What a way to end a vacay, huh?

The gunman directed us with a wave of the pistol. "That's right sit down. Yeah, get situated. No funny stuff. Just get situated."

Right now I hated him more than the kiddie hall monitor who used to poke us in the butt with a ruler if we didn't line up fast enough after recess. And getting down on that floor!

C'mon now.

I hadn't sat on the floor *like this* since what, kindergarten? And I'm in good shape. That's because I make myself work out but not as much as I SHOULD 'cause exercise is H-E-DOUBLE-L on the average black woman's hair. The floor was hard and sitting up straight was pulling on my back. I'd be okay for a while but, on the real, the pregnant lady wasn't gonna last more than a half an hour like this.

The gunman noticed the pregnant woman gingerly attempting to get down on her knees.

"Wait!" he said to her. She froze, drawing her frightened son close to her side.

The gunman backed away toward a padded executive chair with a high back. He grabbed the chair and rolled it toward the pregnant woman. "Sit here." He said it very softly. "I want you to be comfortable."

She sat. "Thank you," she said, then whispered, "What about my son?"

The gunman smiled at the little boy. "Wanna sit on your mommy's lap?"

The little boy was madly sucking on his thumb but nodded a furious yes with his head.

"Go on then," he motioned with his head. "Go on." The boy climbed up on his mother's lap. The gunman said softly to her, "Let me know if you're not comfortable."

The rest of us were already squatted down, taking in this change in personality. Boyfriend's demeanor was just like Chicago weather—if you waited a minute it was sure to change.

He turned around to the rest of us who were now on the floor watching him. The gunman stood over us and began talking to himself—or was it to us? *"I'm thinking,"* he kept repeating. *"I'm thinking."*

Meanwhile I was eyeballing that red sack on the counter with the bomb.

"I'm thinking."

I decided to talk to the man; maybe I could talk him out of doing something crazy. It had already reached the tripped-out stage as it was. But maybe I could stop it before it got downright out of hand.

"What's your name, sir?"

He pointed the gun at me and gaped like I had nine heads and none of 'em the least bit cute. I wasn't talking out of turn though—I had a plan. I'd read this book on hostage situations. I love to read, child. I'll read the label off a fruit can. I've got subscriptions to all the goodies too—*Essence, Newsweek, Sports Illustrated, Upscale*—and when those run out, I hit the books by Eric J. Dickey, Terrie Williams, E. Lynn Harris, Bertice Berry, Tavis Smiley, Connie Briscoe, Francis Ray, Kim Roby, and the crew. When I run out of that, I read my boyfriend Doug's cop manuals and stuff. As a cop with the Chicago P.D.'s ace unit, he's called in to handle any number of things. I've read more books from his classes than a priest reads Scripture.

The one on hostage situations said to try and establish a personal relationship with the suspect; that'll make him more apt to negotiate with you. So I asked my man, AGAIN.

"What's your name, sir?"

"Don't try and trick me, Miss Georgia Barnett. I've seen some of your investigative stories."

Well whoever he was, he watched Channel 8 News. Wonder how that could be worked into one of our commercial promos? How's about something like: *"Channel 8 News: The #1 Choice of Hostage Takers and Bomb Makers."* Don't grab ya? Me neither. But back to the story at hand: I wasn't about to give up. I was REALLY GOING TO HAVE TO work to get a name out of this boy. I kept talking. I couldn't let this scary situation settle over me and knock me off my game.

"But what will we call you? Suppose we have to go to the bathroom or something? I'm just being practical. I'm Georgia and you are . . ."

He pouted his lips before busting out in a goofy grin. One of those *I don't have good sense* grins. "Call me Brett."

Zeke commented. "Like the hockey player Brett Hull. Nice southern name. I'm Zeke."

"You're on borrowed time!" Brett said brandishing the gun in Zeke's direction. "Be quiet."

Then Brett did something weird. He did this Barney Fife impersonation—you know, the skinny country deputy policing the TV town of Mayberry? Him? Well Brett twisted his lips just like old Barn and said in a squeaky voice, "Tick a lock!" Then took an imaginary key and locked his lips before throwing away the key.

Zeke and I looked at each other. The look said, *Ain't this some crazy you-know-what?*

Just as we exchanged this communication, you could hear sirens growing near. Brett kept the gun on us but cocked his head to the side like an old hound hearing a silent dog whistle.

The bank had a big picture window. Normally this would have made it easy for the cops to pick off Brett in a pinch. But because it was summer, the bank employees had pulled down a big sunscreen. *From the inside* you could SEE OUT through a dark blue tint, but the people *on the outside* couldn't SEE IN. They only saw a mirror reflection of themselves and nothing on the inside. I heard car brakes screeching. Doors slamming.

A loud voice came booming over the bullhorn. "This is the police. We have the bank surrounded. Come out with your hands up and no one will get hurt."

Brett coiled his body. I mean you could see him tense up in a knot. From my angle in the hostage pow-wow I could see the cars lining up and then men getting out, guns drawn, bracing themselves against the car hoods.

"Do like they say," the bike messenger warned. "And you'll be all right."

"I don't care about me," Brett said, holding the gun steady. "I'm here for somebody else."

Here for somebody else? *Somebody like who?* How could busting into a bank with a bomb POSSIBLY help somebody else?

Brett pointed his gun at Zeke before rotating it back to me. "You're going to help me."

"Sure," I said. "But why don't you turn yourself in? I CAN REALLY help you on the outside. I promise I'll do all I can no matter what kind of trouble you're in."

"Turn myself in? And get what? Cops and lies. Doctors and lies. No . . . no more. NONE OF THAT. You do like I say, Georgia. I've got a plan. Get your camera."

Suddenly the telephone rang.

We all jerked around in the direction of the ringing phone. It was on a desk near the door, on a right angle from the window.

The phone rang again.

All the hostages cut their eyes at one another. I thought: *The cops are calling trying to get him to the small corner of the window that's exposed.*

Brett kept the gun on us as he slowly sidestepped over to the desk.

Zeke whispered to me, "He picks up that phone, some sharpshooting cop is gonna turn Mr. Bank Robber into loose change."

3

Not change as in nickels and dimes, of course, but CHANGE as in transform or alter, as in reduce homeboy to a splattering *of blood and bone* on the floor in front of us. That would CHANGE our situation for sho', *as in* forever alter our psyche because of the ripping violence we will have just seen.

Lord, *as much* as I wanted to get out of that bank and see everyone else get out of there safe and sound too, I DID NOT WANT to see the man get shot in front of me, *let alone* have it seen by the seven-year-old boy sitting in his mama's lap sucking his thumb.

Brett picked up the phone. His expression didn't change a smidgen. "Lake Michigan Bank." He kept the gun on us.

The guard whispered to Zeke, "I could go for the gun. Can you get his attention?"

"It's too risky now," Zeke whispered back. "We're

sitting ducks on this floor. No way can we all get outta the way if it doesn't work."

Brett spoke to the caller in a monotone. "No."

"I'm gonna try it."

Brett dropped his eyes. "Yes."

"Don't," Zeke said. The guard's hand was between them, partially hidden by their crossed legs. Zeke grabbed the guard's wrist and stuffed his hand underneath his crossed leg and BRACED DOWN HARD.

"Leggo," the guard growled at him.

Brett finished the call. "Okay. I will." He hung up the phone and walked back slowly toward us. His gun was aimed. He walked over to the two tellers.

"Who's Vicki?"

Both women were shaking. I mean they were scared to death and who could half-blame them? I wasn't in the best of shape myself right now. I've learned that the voice within settles the soul, but right now that voice was as steely and quiet as the bank vault just a few feet away.

Brett squatted in front of their faces. "Who's Vicki?"

Instead of answering, the blond held up her hand. It was shaking like a paper bag in the wind.

"Your husband said to bring some milk home for the girls."

Vicki whimpered. I mean she HAD TO have been thinking about her family as it was—then to have something as simple and as fleeting as a call to make a grocery run FORCE HER to think about what she would be losing IF things inside this bank got deadly—was *too much*. Vicki started to cry.

"Don't worry. I don't plan on having a hand in any kids growing up without their mothers. Been there. So just relax." He stood back up.

My mind was going up and down, back and forth about this crazy guy. I mean he comes in with a gun and a bomb, hollering about how he's gonna kill people and blow up the joint. He threatens to blow off the head of my very best cameraman THEN turns around and pampers a pregnant woman AND THEN practically tells a teller that she'll make it home in time to get the kids some milk and cookies.

What the hell is going on here?

"Georgia."

He called my name and I didn't know what to expect, so I readied myself for the unexpected. He could be Mr. Nice or Mr. Nasty.

"Georgia, I want you to show me how to make a tape for TV. I want to send a message to the entire city of Chicago. It's a matter of life or death."

What could I say but "Okay." Then I added, "But I need Zeke. There's no TV without a cameraman."

Once again the bullhorn blared, "You inside. Come out with your hands up and no one will get hurt."

Brett acted like he didn't hear it. He motioned with his gun for Zeke to get up.

Slowly he did. For the first time in years I took a nice, long look at Zeke Rouster. He's about 5'10" with stone white hair and pale green eyes. Zeke's long, spindly legs looked pretty frail as he got up off the floor, his jelly belly being his center of gravity. He wore the standard cameraman gear. Jeans. Polo shirt. Work boots. Baseball cap.

The phone rang AGAIN.

This time Brett looked angry. He pointed the gun at me. "You answer it. I KNOW it's the police now. Tell them if they cut the phones or the lights, I'll blow up the joint. Tell them I don't wanna talk now. I'll be sending out a taped message shortly. Everything they need to know will be on it."

Brett was being Mr. Nasty. I didn't respond.

"GOT IT? NOW GET THE PHONE."

I answered the call. "Hello. This is Georgia Barnett. Channel 8 News."

"This is District Commander Bill Whelk."

I closed my eyes and cussed my unlucky stars. WILD BILL Whelk. He had moved up through the ranks of the Chicago P.D. like a bad brush fire. That's because he came from a long line of cops. They pulled strings for him, but don't tell him that UNLESS you're looking to get cussed out. *Wild Bill was the kind of guy who was born on third base and thought he hit a triple.*

He also had a rep, not just for being tough, which the average reporter would appreciate and the average citizen would love—but for being a publicity hog. If there was a high-profile case where the brass could catch a shower of glory, Wild Bill would be standing there BUTT NAKED bathing in it, singing a *funky falsetto* of the Bee Gees' "Staying Alive."

Because of this, Wild Bill had a mixed following on the force. Some hated his guts and others were loyal. Those who were loyal admired his take-charge attitude. Plus he went to the right events. You always saw him at the Chicago Police Academy graduation and the fund-raisers for the families of fallen cops. The man didn't miss a thing and every now and then when he was trying to hog the spotlight, he'd pull in an average Joe Flatfoot to catch a ray or two of the spotlight as well.

But behind the scenes, where I had watched him work, the man was ruthless. Took no prisoners. Word was that Wild Bill had his eye on politics. Cool. That's right where a shark belongs—*where there's always some blood in the water.*

"Are you on the line by yourself, Georgia?"

"Yes," I answered. I'd worked enough high-profile crime stories that the two of us were on a first-name basis. "Bill, I've been told to give you and your officers a message."

Brett was staring me in the face so hard that you would have SWORN the boy was deaf and trying to read my lips.

"Georgia, let me talk to the gunman. Right now!"

"He won't come to the phone . . ."

I rolled my eyes. *He don't wanna talk to you and I'm not trying to get him mad, okay?*

"He doesn't want to talk now. He'll be sending out a videotaped message shortly. If you cut the phone lines or the lights, he'll blow the place up. Just wait for the video-tape."

"What is this, some silly media stunt? I HOPE you aren't steering him in that direction to get some kinda crazy exclusive? 'Cause I'm not letting it happen, Georgia."

Wasn't that enough to make a sister wanna cuss him four different ways 'til Sunday? Like I told this man to walk into the bank with a GUN and a BOMB and turn everybody's life upside down so I could get a story on the air? In a word: *ignorant.*

I looked at Brett, who had started sweating and was clearly getting impatient. He started to rock back and forth ever so slightly.

"The gunman is in control," I said, looking right at Brett. "He wants you to stop yelling on the bullhorn and stop calling. He will communicate with police but ONLY by videotaped message, which he'll be sending out shortly. This is what he's told me to tell you."

"The customers who got out said there was a pregnant woman and a kid in there. Is that true?"

"Yes."

"The gunman has a bomb?"

"Yes."

"You guys hang tight. We'll get the son of a bitch."

"Right."

Brett lunged toward me, grabbed the phone out of my hand, and slammed it down into the cradle. "What'd he say—what'd he say?"

I stayed cool. Being cool is the only way to deal with a situation like this. My face was *Mama Cool* but my stomach was churning and my throat was having its own private drought. I told myself, *He's sensitive, Georgia. He hates cops. So make him think Wild Bill was the bad guy on the phone. Let him know you were obedient. Lives are depending on it.*

"It's not my fault, Brett. I wanted to tell him what you said and nothing more. But it was him. He kept barking questions at me, just like he did at you over the bullhorn."

Brett calmed down and looked kinda sympathetic. "What did he wanna know?"

Stress does some crazy stuff to you. A song popped

into my head. Swear before the Lord. I heard that old
'70s tune "Get Down Tonight" by K.C. and The Sunshine
Band in my head. I kept the chorus and made up a lyric
in my head.

*Tell a little lie, tell a little truth, do a little dance—get
down tonight, get down tonight.*

I thought fast. "He wanted to know if everybody
was all right. I said yes. Then he wanted to know if there
was a pregnant woman and a child in here and I said
yes. Then he asked me if all the police should do is wait
'til you tell them what to do next and I said right."

"Okay," Brett shrugged. "That's okay." He relaxed.
"Now show me how to make the tape."

"First, we have to decide how we're going to shoot
it." When I said shoot, my eyes dropped right down to
his gun. I quickly glanced back up. "Do you want to sit
or stand?"

The hostage in the business suit groused, "I don't
believe this!"

Zeke backhanded him with a dirty look. Then he
glanced at me and quickly suggested, "How about he
takes a seat with some light?"

What's Zeke up to now?

I watched him walk around me and stop at the desk
where I had stood and taken the phone call, right by the
window, away from the bomb on the counter and a short
distance away from the hostage powwow. Zeke held his
hands out by the desk, "See? The light's good here, Georgia."

When I turned to look, Zeke whispered, "We get
him over here away from everybody else and I'll jump
him."

Brett wasn't to be played. "I'll stand here by the hostages. With my gun. And get the bomb in the picture next to me."

Zeke and I shared a look. *Mr. Stickup Man has turned Spielberg on us.*

"But the light is better here, Brett," Zeke tried in vain.

Brett kicked a small black box with the words PORTABLE LIGHTS on it. "You've got equipment, use it."

As soon as he said that, THE UNEXPECTED HAPPENED. The situation exploded. All *you-know-what* broke loose. The bike messenger kid pulled a gun out of his shin guards, aimed, and FIRED.

I've always hated guns with a passion. It's not a girl thing either. I know some women, AND THEY ARE NOT COPS, who can shoot their butts off and love the sport of it. These are some *baaad girls* who can heft a piece and do some real damage on the shooting range.

Now, I can shoot too. Had a great-uncle who taught me one summer while I was visiting my people down south. Between learning how to make blackberry cobbler from scratch and shooting an empty RC can off a tree stump, I was stressed out to the max that sweet sixteen summer. No joke.

The thing I disliked the most was the sound that the gun made. Silly enough, it was because of the way every animal in the woods scattered at the first crack. Every bird and every grasshopper, the crickets, all of those animals just scattered when we started those shooting lessons. Any other time? When some of us kids would take a walk by the stream, we'd see a rabbit or nest full of birds, raccoons even. But once all the animals cleared out, those beautiful woods seemed lifeless and haggard, burdened by absence, laden with fear, and us, the visitors rude enough to clear the forest family out of what God had given them as their own.

The sound just put everything that had a heart and drew breath on edge—including me. Wanting to hurry up and get it right, I would knock the stew out of those cans on the first round so my great-uncle would do his Beverly Hillbilly laugh and say, "Mercy." Then maybe he'd *have mercy* and we could go home earlier. He wasn't having it, explaining in that long, snaking drawl of his the reasoning behind our gun lessons.

"Ya see. All girls . . . and especially pretty ones like you, city or southern, Georgia, need to know how to shoot and to drive the bejesus out of a car including a stick shift. Might have to get away from somebody quick and in some kinda hurry one day." He aimed with the gun and punked every single crushed can bent and wobbling on top of that hacked-up stump. "I want my womenfolk to be ready for some of anything. Times are changing. *Mercy*."

I could hear his voice say "Mercy" right after I heard that gunshot crackle through the stifling, plastic commercial air of the bank.

Something else you have to remember about guns too. And that's the fact that they can go off and do their own thing. YOU THINK you're aiming at a tin can. You exhale at the wrong time and you wind up putting a bullet in the gut of a nearby tree or it grazes the tree and ricochets and hits the side of a pickup truck. Or worse . . . God, as many times as we've all heard this, someone picks up the gun and holds it the wrong way. Like a mad, jilted lover that gun DOES NOT like how it's being held and it snaps. Pops off. Hates on the holder and lets fly with all the power and the pinned-up fire that's burning in its chambers, sending a bullet spinning out of control, hitting and tearing into someone else, sending flesh flying . . .

That's what the bike messenger had hoped to do when he reached for the gun that he had hidden in his shin guard. Why did he have a gun hidden there anyway? Why take a chance and pull it now? Was he a good enough shot to *hit Brett* and save us all? Or would he *miss Brett* and Brett turn right around and take him out? OR WORSE *even still*, would Brett detonate the bomb and blow us all up?

Mercy.

That bullet whizzed by and all the hostages doubled over and covered their heads. The tellers were screaming. I was frozen in my tracks. Waiting . . .

It missed.

It missed Brett and lodged in the oak paneling beneath the tellers' window. That's because Brett dived out of the way, lunging across the floor. Brett landed two feet away from the bike messenger, his gun hand raised, pointed at the messenger's temple.

"Drop it," Brett ordered.

The bike messenger did.

"If anybody even looks like they wanna move, I'll blow their brains out."

The little boy was sobbing loudly now as his mother clutched him to her bosom. She rocked back and forth in the chair.

Brett got up slowly, still aiming at the bike messen-

ger's skull. He took his free hand and slapped the bike
helmet off the guy's head and pressed the barrel of the
gun RIGHT UP AGAINST the young man's temple. The
bike messenger began to pray in Spanish in a low voice.
Brett picked up the pistol that had failed to take his life.
He stuffed it into the belt of his pants.

The phone rang.

Brett's head snapped around and his eyes squinted
in anger.

"It's okay," I said shakily. "I'll get rid of them."

I wanted Brett to think he could trust me, that I was
on his side. In his mind, Zeke had already betrayed him.
The bank guard too. Now this messenger kid. I couldn't
let him lose faith in me. Our lives depended on it.

I yanked up the phone receiver. "What's your problem? We said no more telephone calls."

"All right," Wild Bill grumped. "Jesus H. Christ. We
heard a gunshot."

"No!" I lied to Wild Bill. "There was no gunshot." I
looked over at Brett. He was buying my act. "We know if
you hear gunshots you might come tearing in here and
NOBODY wants that. Bye."

Brett was breathing out of his mouth now. His eyes
were darting back and forth. The low murmur of fluent
Spanish hummed in the air like a hovering bee.

"Whatya trying to pull?" Brett yelled at the bike
messenger. "What's with the gun? Answer me or so help
me . . ."

"I needed protection! Okay? I've been getting
robbed left and right."

Brett had no sympathy for the man. "*So what . . . I
oughta kill you.*"

The bike messenger closed his eyes again and re-sumed his prayer. Big drops of perspiration printed a pattern around the edge of his ears.

Brett went to another place within himself, fearless of what our eyes might see or our ears might hear or more importantly what our hearts might judge.

"You have no idea what my life has been. I'm trying to hold on here. I'm trying to save the one good thing in my life and you're making it harder. Don't you get it? I don't need NOTHING or NOBODY to make my life harder than it's already been. Now I'm tired of being beat down, of being scared. I'm taking charge and fighting back and any-body who gets in my way and wants to beat me down or make me feel scared is going straight to hell so help me God."

I heard the gun cock. Anticipation of the moment settled over me.

"Wait a minute, friend," Zeke said. "The kid made a mistake. Why that little old popgun he had COULDN'T hurt a tough guy like you. Why it would only sting ya."

Zeke went into his heavy good-old-boy act. Turned it on to disarm folks. I've seen him pull it off in the crazi-est of places. And God knows this place had turned NOTHING BUT crazy on an ordinary day.

Zeke drawled. "And let me tell ya. A sting by a 'Bama skeeter will hurt you worse than that little old popgun. 'Bama skeeter bite will make your arm darn near fall off. I remember one time . . ."

"All right!" Brett yelled at Zeke. Then he took the gun away from the bike messenger's temple. "You. Get up!"

My heart began beating against the walls of my chest like a kid who'd accidentally locked herself in a closet.

Brett walked the man over to a large room. You could see the safety-deposit boxes lining the walls. Brett whacked him upside the head with the butt of the gun, shoved him inside, and closed the metal door. The latch locked with a heavy thunk. Then he rushed back over to us.

"The next person that tries something won't get locked up, they're going to get taken out. And I mean it. Understand?"

Our silence was fearful affirmation.

"Now, no more games. I've gotta make that tape." Brett looked at the teller whose husband called about bringing home some milk for the kids. "Vicki, what's in the staff lounge?"

Brett's question drew all of our attention to the door across the way from the ladies' bathroom.

Vicki struggled to find her voice.

Time for a Brett personality change. "Just tell me the truth. I won't hurt you. Is it a big room or a small room?"

Vicki's voice crept out, bending and cracking. "Kinda small."

"What's in there?"

"A couch. A television . . . uh . . . the microwave and a coffee maker."

"A TV? Good." Brett nodded. "That'll do. Is there a big room around here?"

Vicki was shaking, growing more and more nervous.

"Talk to me. Is there a conference room or something?"

Vicki raised her hand and pointed. We all followed her lead and turned toward a room that could clearly be seen over the waist-high wood counter to our left. It was a pretty big room with a round table and several chairs. There were no windows leading to the outside world and it was glass from floor to ceiling facing the interior of the bank.

"How many phones in there?"

Vicki held up her index finger.

"Does the door lock?"

Vicki nodded yes.

"Where's the key?"

Vicki's eyes slid over to the bank security guard. We all looked at him, our gaze landing on the key ring attached to his belt.

"Good. Okay. One at a time as I point to you: get up, step forward, and empty out your pockets or your purse."

One by one, all of us did as Brett asked. Dumping money and cell phones, credit cards, candy, cigarettes, lighters, and whatnot. The seven-year-old even gave up his yo-yo.

"Good. Guard, give me your keys."

The guard reached out his hand.

"Stop!" Brett ordered.

The guard flipped his hand over and motioned as if to pitch the keys to Brett.

"Stop." Brett nodded downward. "On the floor and slide them over with the side of your foot. Easily like."

The security guard did as he was told.

Brett picked up the keys. "Which one?"

"They're marked."

Brett nodded. "I see." He picked the key out and let the rest dangle on the ring. "Let's go." Brett motioned with the gun. "Hands in the air. Single file into the conference room."

We all walked over to the conference room. Brett sent the guard in first.

"Rip the phone jack out of the wall."

The guard did.

"Good. Now the rest of you get in there. Quick."

Zeke and I were the last two with Brett holding the gun to our backs. Everyone else made it into the room, but when Zeke started to enter, Brett stopped him.

"Not you and Georgia."

He gave Zeke the key. "Lock 'em in." Zeke closed the conference room door and locked it.

"Gimme the key." Zeke handed Brett the keys. He stuffed them in his back pocket. "Now that they're out of the way, let's make TV."

5

So what do you make of this guy so far? Me? I didn't HAVE A CLUE where he was going with all this. Brett now had TWO GUNS and a BOMB. His moods swung higher than a kiddie swing on the playground. Mean one minute. Accommodating the next. He didn't trust the guys. But he did seem to trust the girls—at least he trusted the teller Vicki and me. He hadn't mentioned stealing any money. And this had to be about the almighty dollar, didn't it? Like the O-Jays sing, *You can do thangs, bad thangs with it.*

But my man—or should I say my menace—Brett had declared that he was here for somebody else. Then he said something about it being a matter of life or death. And he wanted to send a videotaped message to the world, to make TV with the help of Zeke and me.

None of it was making a lick of sense but what could we do?

We stood Brett up by the teller counter. Zeke set up

the lights, putting them on the floor, aimed up at Brett.
He tilted them left so there wouldn't be a shadow on his
face. Finally, Zeke went behind Brett and put up a piece
of flat material on a metal stand that would bounce the
light back down and give a sunshine effect.

Zeke handed me a clip-on mike.

I walked over to Brett. His eyes narrowed. "What
are you doing?"

I held up the clip-on mike, which looks like a small
black button attached to a hair clip dragging a long tail
behind it. "Silent films went out with the Great Depression. You need this mike and I have to put it on for you,
unless you know how?"

Not that I wanted to get close to this knucklehead at
all. But the way his mood was swinging back and forth, I
wanted this videotape to turn out right. No telling what
this fool might do if something went wrong.

"Okay. But no tricks."

"Have I been anything but straight with you?" I
asked. He nodded and pouted like my little nephew Zack
when I'd call him on all the whining he tried to do whenever I told him "no." Zack would whine that *Auntie never
took him anywhere.* Then his little face would crack
AFTER I'd rattle off all the movies, baseball games, and
museums I had just taken him to.

"Okay," I told Brett. "Let's get you miked up."

I slid the wire through a loop in his belt buckle
and ran it under his arm, around his back, over his
shoulder and clipped it onto his shirt just below his
chin. Doing that, I glimpsed a piece of folded-up paper
in his pocket. My eyes caught a disturbing headline:
POLICE ALERT.

I thought quickly. "Lose this paper. It's going to be in the shot and won't look good."

I took it out of his pocket and tossed it onto the counter like I didn't care about it. It opened a little bit. I could see that it REALLY was a POLICE ALERT. There was a sketch of a suspect on it too. Was it Brett? Was he a wanted man? If it was, what was he wanted for? Cops put out alerts shortly after a crime, when they have a good description of a suspect and the case is still hot.

I racked my brain quickly.

There hadn't been any bank robberies in the city or the surrounding suburbs lately. So I had to put an X on my theory that this drama was part of a bank-robbing spree. What other kind of dirt was this guy capable of doing?

"All right," Zeke said, getting Brett's attention. "Look here." He held his hand up just over the top of the camera that he had mounted onto the tripod. "Just above the camera eye."

Brett was stone-faced.

"Relax," I said.

I needed to take my own advice. I kept looking back at the BIG RED SACK on the counter with the bomb in it. I didn't have a clue what the explosive device looked like. And when I had gotten close to Brett I didn't see any kind of device in his pocket or in his hand. How could he possibly detonate that thing from afar? *Was he bluffing?*

Zeke wanted to test the audio. "Mike check," he said.

Brett looked confused, then smiled. "I love green eggs and ham Sam I am."

Zeke and I cut our eyes at each other. Was this guy off? Or was he trying to run a game on us? I wasn't quite sure what was going down. Zeke? He didn't tip his hand *either way*, just pushed forward with the business of making the tape.

"Your audio is good. I'll roll off a little bit of tape, then I'll point to you. That's your cue to start talking: say whatcha gotta say."

Brett aimed his gun at me. "Get back next to the camera guy where I can see you. No funny stuff."

I began backing up . . . slowly . . . slowly.

Brett stopped me short. "Wait. Give me that newspaper I saw over there. On that desk."

I looked around and spotted the paper. I moved to give it to Brett, but he shook his head.

"Turn to the weather and see what time sunset is."

I did as he asked, a bit baffled, but what other choice did I have. "Says 8:20 P.M."

Brett nodded. "Good. That's the deadline. If I don't get my daughter back by that time I'm gonna blow this joint up."

I cringed.

"Now," Brett ordered, "put the newspaper down and get me that paper you took out of my pocket and tried to read on the sly."

Everything slick don't slide. I hadn't gotten away with as much as I thought. Brett was calling a sister out about trying to take a sneak peek at the police alert.

I stepped up to the counter and picked up the paper. Brett took it with his free hand and shook it open. With his gun hand he waved me over by Zeke. "Go ahead. Back up."

I backpedaled over by Zeke. Zeke pointed at Brett and said, "Go."

BRETT THE BANK ROBBER *was on*.

"Hello. Most of you people out there watching don't know me. You think I'm a bad man because I'm holding hostages in this bank. But I'm here to help somebody else. I'm a parent just like a lot of you watching. My daughter is in trouble. Her name is Mandy. My little girl is with THIS MAN."

Brett held up the police alert.

"This is a wanted poster that police put out on him. He's a robber AND a drug dealer; he's got my little girl and no one would believe me or help me. Not the doctors or the police. So now I'm not asking for help. I'm demanding it. The police have to find my daughter. Get Mandy away from this guy. I know he's gonna hurt her. I WANT MY LITTLE GIRL SAFE, UNDERSTAND. And if I see Mandy outside the bank and she tells me she's safe, I'll let the hostages go. If not, I'll blow this bank up and everybody in it. You have until 8:20 P.M. to find her. That's it."

Brett's voice cracked.

"And to my little girl, if you're out there watching. Daddy is going to fix it, baby. Don't worry. I'll fix it."

Then Brett looked over at Zeke. "That's it. That's all I've got to say. We'll send that out and have the cops put that on the tube. That oughta do it."

Zeke asked, "What about the poster? You plan on sending that out?"

Brett shook his head no. "I need that to remember the guy."

Huh? I thought. He couldn't remember the man he was trying to protect his daughter from?

"Brett," I said, "the police will need more information. How did this guy get your daughter? Where did he live last? What does your daughter look like? How old is she?"

Why did I start asking questions? Brett got pissed: madder than Al Sharpton at a Moral Majority meeting. A burst of crimson exploded in his cheeks. Then little beads of sweat formed at the corner of his mouth. "I don't know. How do you expect me to remember all that?" His eyes got teary. "The police have to find her. That's all I want . . . That's all . . . Is that too much to ask?"

"Okay. Okay." I tried to calm him down. "They'll find her."

Zeke jumped in and tried to defuse the situation too. "Hold up that wanted poster so I can get a good shot of it on tape."

Brett held it up. Zeke zoomed in on it. After a few seconds he said, "Got it." Then Zeke popped the tape.

"Okay," Brett ordered. "We'll toss it out to the cops and they'll put it on TV."

I had to take a chance here. I had to try to get something more out of Brett. Could I get him to spring a hostage?

"Brett, if you just toss the tape out of the door, they'll take it. Sure. But maybe they won't really do anything with it. Cops are pushy. Remember how they were on the phone?"

Brett nodded.

"Well maybe they'd be more likely to work better if you send it out with a hostage."

"You're trying to trick me."

"No I'm not. Let a hostage, like the pregnant woman and her son, take it out. That would be a sign of good faith, wouldn't it?"

Brett thought a moment.

"Okay." He aimed the gun at me. "But not her and the kid. They're the best hostages I got. Get the teller, Vicki." Brett tossed me the keys. "Let her out. The conference room key is marked. Pull anything funny and video man over here gets a bullet."

I took the keys and began walking back to the conference room. I held my breath, and the key ring in front of me. I walked slowly, my eyes down at the key ring. When I searched for the conference room key, I spotted one next to it marked, "garage door." *Jackpot.* I slipped it off the ring.

When Brett had us looking around at the conference room and the staff lounge, I noticed the door in the rear that was marked, "Garage Exit." Zeke and I parked in the outside lot. But on several occasions I've parked in the underground garage that the bank shares with some of the other nearby shops. I dropped the key on the floor by the security guard. We made eye contact but he didn't look down. I turned to Vicki.

"Vicki?" I said. "Come with me."

Her eyes got wide with fear.

"It's okay. C'mon." She whimpered and stood up. "It's going to be okay."

Vicki followed me out. "What's going on? What's happening?"

"Relax. You're getting out of here."

Girlfriend broke down and started bawling. We reached Brett and he handed Vicki the tape. "Tell them to play it on TV now. And find my daughter. If they don't, I'll BLOW UP the joint."

Vicki's hand was shaking so much I thought she was gonna drop the tape. She turned and began walking toward the door.

"Hey," Brett shouted.

Vicki turned and looked.

"Don't forget the milk for the kids."

A tear rolled down Vicki's face as she whimpered, "Thank you."

6

Vicki was grateful. But we were worried.

Half an hour passed; it was 10:15 A.M.

Brett was pacing back and forth, mumbling to himself. He made Zeke unhook the TV in the lounge and bring it out into the bank lobby. Brett had Zeke prop it up on some loan officer's desk. He aimed that remote like a laser beam, zapping from channel to channel.

Zeke and I were back doing the hostage powwow on the floor. Why hadn't the television stations played the tape? In TV you can interrupt a broadcast in a few minutes. Why hadn't they done that? And it's always about competition on a story, too. ABC *wanted to beat* CBS who *wanted to beat* NBC who *wanted to take it to* Fox and *so on and so on* . . .

"What's the problem?" Brett whined. "I don't see it. Where's my tape?"

Brett was talking more to himself than to Zeke and me. I knew that because boyfriend was speaking low and made no eye contact *whatsoever* with either one of us. Meanwhile Zeke and I were whispering back and forth.

"Zeke, when I let Vicki out, I slipped the garage key off the ring and dropped it on the floor by the guard."

"Did he see it?"

"Yeah."

"Lot of good it'll do. They're locked up in that conference room."

"But if he ever lets them out again, and we get a chance to go after him, they can make a run for that door."

Brett shouted at us, "Hey! What are you talking about?"

When you're a TV reporter, thinking fast on your feet is a must, baby. You could be doing a live shot somewhere and some knucklehead wannabe gets in the shot shouting, "Hi Mom!" And you have to recover. So when Brett shot the question at us, survival mode kicked in and the brain started spitting out the right answers to appease this angry gunman who was trying in a desperately wrong way to help his daughter.

"Me and Zeke were trying to figure out what was taking so long for them to play the tape."

Brett blustered. "Did you mess up something?"

"Hell no," Zeke huffed. *Bravado works with a bad man y'all.* Brett calmed down. Then a worried look yawned across his face as he asked, "Then what, Georgia?"

"Well, all the television stations will want a copy. Cable too. Like CNN. That takes time to dub the tape and send it out to everybody." I was rolling. Then I decided to do an A-1 ego stroke. "Then they're all probably trying to get their big anchors in place. This is an important story. This is no little piddly deal here, right? Everybody needs to know this is a priority. To get Mandy back—nothing's more important than that, right?" I was stroking this boy's ego something fierce. *Had I been in water, I'd be on pace to set an Olympic record.* "And Brett, I watched you make the tape. You were good."

"Real good." Zeke chimed in. "Might have a future in TV, man."

I narrowed my eyes at Zeke, willing him to hear my thoughts. *Don't go overboard now. You're gonna mess around and get us killed.*

Brett had parked the TV on my station, Channel 8. I saw the slate come up. "Look," I said, motioning with my head. The screen was filled with a blue background that read SPECIAL REPORT.

Pete, one of our top reporters but not *an anchor,* had been grabbed up to do an emergency cut-in. That's when they can't find a regular anchor and they need somebody with a reporter's union card to go on air to be the first with a story. Even if you said, "Details are sketchy but Boo-Boo the Fool is doing X," JUST THAT was enough to give you bragging rights over the competition. Here's how it played with Pete.

We interrupt this broadcast to bring you a special report.

Channel 8 News has learned of a hostage situation at Lake Michigan Bank.

Details are sketchy but here's what we do know: there is at least one gunman and more than six hostages.

We will bring you updates on this breaking story as soon as they become available.

Channel 8's Georgia Barnett is live at the scene.

Live at the scene? *I'm a hostage.* WHAT'S UP WITH THAT? They had to know. Why not report it? Brett surfed to another channel. The competition was doing a cut-in too. Same thing. Hostages. No names. Details are sketchy. Why not more? Out of all the people who ran out of the bank—those lucky dogs—you CAN'T TELL ME they didn't all *bark and howl at the moon* about who was inside. The cops knew about the pregnant woman and her son. Wild Bill told me that . . . and . . .

Aww shoot. As my grandma would say, *Sucky-sucky now. There's some dirt in the game.*

The ONLY person who could squash this and keep these stations in the dark is Wild Bill. But why hold back on those details and why not play the tape? A bold and deadly statement by Brett interrupted my thoughts.

"I'm gonna have to shoot somebody," Brett said, shaking his head. "That's the only damn way they'll take me seriously. They're gonna make me shoot somebody. Do you understand that Georgia, huh?"

Nooooo and ain't tryin' to understand either. Don't look at me and say you gotta shoot somebody. *Please.* Cut those big criminal eyes at somebody who'll fall in love with you. Not me. And don't aim them at my right-hand man, my backup, my boy Zeke either.

"Brett, you don't have to do that."

"Yeah I do. Mandy is in trouble and these people won't help. I ask for help and NOBODY is helping because they think I'm *a joke;* that all of this is some kinda crazy game. So I've gotta shoot somebody to make them move. That'll light a fire under their butts."

Brett aimed his gun at me.

I didn't hold my breath; breath just stop coming. My *"I want my mommy"* lungs were clutching each other and shivering inside my chest and my nerves weren't a bit more courageous. The hairs on the back of my neck were standing on end; *couldn't have been any straighter if they had been pressed with a hot comb by Madam C. J. Walker herself.*

"Eenie," Brett said, then moved the gun to Zeke, "meanie . . ."

Yeah. The random kid game. Eenie. Meanie. Minie. Moe.

The last time somebody played that game on me was oh, I'd say, more than thirty years ago. That somebody was my twin sister Peaches, now a blues-singing, fire-breathing single parent. We were playing out on a fire escape in our Englewood neighborhood on the south side. At the time Peaches and I were only seven. Peaches was a *bossy big mama.* Pudgy but with plenty of pride, and me, skinny and gullible, I let her talk me into pooling all our money for candy.

That's bad enough.

Then I let Peaches talk me into playing this game, WINNER TAKE ALL. Whoever wound up being Moe was the winner.

Gullible me. Who knew that you could actually start the song and ADD OR SUBTRACT lyrics to make Moe land on *whomever* you wanted? Simple math. And what made it *soooo bad?* Peaches' sassy seven-year-old self was singing the kiddie rhyme like a hard-core street-walker . . . and shaking her shimmy too. I got so tickled every time that I didn't realize 'til her jaws were sticking out like a chipmunk's that she had conned me out of my share of the candy. I ALWAYS LOST AT EENIE . . . MEANIE . . . MINIE . . . MOE.

So do I have to tell you? No, I'm sure I don't. But ah sistah will. I AM NOT a fan of Eenie. Meanie. Minie. Moe.

So before he got to the part about catching a tiger, *and we don't mean Woods,* by the toe, I just stopped Brett the bank robber cold.

"Send me out. I'll get that tape on air. I promise."

"You're trying to trick me."

"Swear to God who is my savior I'm not. I'll get that tape on. I'll do everything I can to find your daughter too. I've got two Emmys for investigative reporting and have more contacts than an eye doctor."

Brett stopped pointing the gun at Zeke and then pointed it straight up at the ceiling, falling into deep thought. "That could work." He turned away from us, walked over by the bomb and fingered the big red sack with his free hand. Then Brett began to rock a bit.

Zeke whispered, *"He's gonna do it. He's gonna let you out of here."*

Brett turned around and came back over to us. He seemed so intimidating standing over us although he was a slight man. He ran his hand through his hair and the lines around his mouth twitched. "My daughter is all I got. I love her and I'm scared for her. Help me. Don't let them people out there force me to do things I don't wanna. I have to trust that you'll get that tape on."

"I'll come through."

"You'd better, Georgia. AND I only want to talk to you. That's it. You can communicate back by TV—like that guy we just saw on your station? Those whatchamacallit things—"

"Newsbreaks?"

"Right. We'll talk back and forth by tape, you and me, Georgia. If things get rotten, and you don't do your part and the police don't do theirs and find Mandy, the world will know that whatever bad happens, it's not my fault."

"Okay." I stood up.

"Now I want you to get that tape on in ten minutes."

"Brett, you've gotta give me longer than that."

"Don't con me."

"I'm not. I can get it on Channel 8's air in a heartbeat. BUT like I said, to dub and send it out to all the other stations is a lot of legwork and so it will take some time. I need more time." It was clear he was thinking. He rubbed his chest with his free hand. His black sweatshirt shifted up and down, making it look like the blue sea horse on his chest was swimming.

"We want to find Mandy, right?"

"That's all," Brett whispered. "Never wanted the rest of this. I'm just trying to save my daughter."

"Okay then." I was begging like a poor whore begs a pimp. "Please . . . please . . . give me some time. Give me an hour."

"Okay. I'll give you an hour. But UNDERSTAND if I think ANYBODY is pulling something funny, your friend here is the first to take a bullet."

"I hear you loud and clear." I took a deep breath.

"Can I talk to the hostages before I go to let them know what's going on?"

Brett shook his head no. "The less they know the better for them."

"Can I hug my cameraman?"

Brett nodded.

Zeke began to get up. He reached his knees.

"Far enough," Brett cautioned.

Zeke and I looked at each other before embracing. He hadn't shaved and was toying with the idea of growing a beard. "Ya know, I think you oughta lose the beard. With your southern accent, you're starting to remind me of Jed Clampett."

Ordinarily Zeke would let out that gorgeous laugh of his, then come right back and crack on me. His eyes glistened. Couldn't tell if they were glistening with *tears or from fear.* I hugged him again.

"Georgia. Promise you won't call my wife. I don't want her cutting her trip short and coming home or worrying herself sick. She waited a long time for this cruise. Besides, what can she do? Don't you call her unless—"

"Zeke, I can't promise something like that."

"You promise me, girl." Zeke's eyes narrowed. "I'm the one staying. I'm the one at risk, Georgia. You gotta honor my wishes. Now promise me."

What could I do? What could I say? "I promise."

"All right then. You won't contact my wife unless—"

"There's not gonna be an unless, Zeke."

Zeke nodded, his eyes showing the beginning glow of confidence. "You know what you gotta do."

"Enough already," Brett said, cutting off our conversation.

But I wasn't having it. "I know."

"Follow your gut and don't worry about me."

Brett began pushing me toward the door.

"Hey Zeke," I yelled over Brett's shoulder, trying to joke 'cause who knew? Maybe I would never see him again. "Remember, Brett wants to communicate by video. None of that lazy stuff. I want clean, clear video or I'm gonna get you fired!"

He yelled back. "Don't worry, Georgia. I plan on being fearless and focused."

Blessed are those who focus, for they shall not be rattled.

Follow along with the drama. *And ah one* . . . I had to make sure the TV stations played the tape. *And ah two* . . . I had to make sure Wild Bill and the Chicago P.D. boys looked for Mandy. *And ah three* . . . I still didn't trust them so I was going to have to look myself . . .

Brett threw open the door of the bank and shouted, "Don't shoot. Hostage coming out."

I kicked my hips into high gear, baby, and ran for the safety line filled with the boys in blue. I made it with ease. My feet felt light because some of the burden of fear had been lifted. I no longer had to worry about my safety.

ONLY ZEKE'S, AND EVERY OTHER HOSTAGE'S IN THAT BANK.

The cops grabbed me and hustled me over to an ambulance. They had on so much S.W.A.T. gear I could hardly see their faces. I was heaving air in and out of my

YOLANDA JOE

mouth. It was difficult to talk. Everything around me was moving in slow motion although in my mind I knew we were racing across the street. I concentrated and forced my throat to propel the words I needed to get out. To my surprise, I didn't sound desperate. I sounded direct.

"I've got to see Bill Whelk, now."

"You'd better get checked out first."

"But—"

The S.W.A.T. guy ignored me and began dragging me over to the back of the ambulance. Once there he lifted me up and plopped me on the table inside. I glanced up and spotted a mirror they had propped up in the corner. I got a good look at myself.

Now when I left the house at dawn, this black woman was in *fine mode*. I'm on air. Had to have my hair together. Had to have my Fashion Fair face on. Had to have on my Tahari pants suit. *Bang. Lights, camera, news.* I'm not bragging, just laying down the laws of the TV trade: a female reporter must look good. So I started out on a roll, but now my roll had turned into a *whirl of whupdom.*

What's whupdom?

Whupdom is when you've been running around so much that you wind up looking crazy. Sometimes I looked like that after covering a fire. Sometimes I looked like that after covering a flood. Right now my hair was standing on top of my head from when I tussled around on the floor with the other hostages. My light suit was dirty ALL OVER, plus bloody on one sleeve from the cut Zeke got trying to take Brett on. My Marvelous Mauve lipstick had left my lips and streaked all along my cheek.

The paramedic dude took my blood pressure and said, "It's high."

No *Sweet'N Low*, Sherlock. YOURS would be *high as a flag* TOO if you had just come out of a situation where every *two seconds on the Timex* some man was sticking a GUN in your face or threatening to blow you up with a BOMB. *Please.*

"Any bruises?" the paramedic asked.

"I don't have time for this!" I dry heaved.

"Any bruises?"

"No. Not really. Got a scrape on my hand from rolling around on the floor but that's it."

"Feel faint?"

"I *feel* fed up. I have to see Bill Whelk. *Now.*"

"Your blood pressure is pretty high. And you have a slight fever. Stress can trigger that. You'd better take it easy for a minute, just sit here for a while."

I whipped off my dirty, bloody jacket and tied it tomboy fashion around my waist. I pushed the paramedic back and slid off the table. "I'm out of here. I've got a man with a gun and a bomb willing to kill one of my best friends, not to mention a bunch of other folks, INCLUDING a pregnant woman and a little boy. Now stand clear."

I took two quick steps and hopped down out of the ambulance. The two S.W.A.T. boys who had helped me into the ambulance in the first place jerked around. I barked at them like a drill sergeant, "My mama raised me right. I don't believe in hunting NO MAN DOWN. But this is a MATTER OF LIFE OR DEATH. Now are you gonna take me to Bill Whelk or am I going to have to find him myself?"

Less than a minute later I was standing grill to grill with Wild Bill Whelk. *And he is not a looker y'all.* If he were a piece of wood, Wild Bill would be a four-by-four. Dude is big and thick. He always wore his hat, guess 'cause it added an inch or two to his 5'5" height. Saw him take off the hat once; that was at the police academy graduation when they sang "God Bless America." He had a crew cut. That went well with his *Popeye the Sailor Man* chin and tight gaze. He had a charged, baritone voice. And that's what he greeted me with.

"Well, well," Wild Bill said. "Ms. Barnett. I'll bet you've seen better days."

That's the essence of Wild Bill. He likes to signify. Anybody else with a heart *instead of a tin can* in the middle of his chest would have said, "How are you feeling?" Or, "Glad you made it out alive." Not this *T. J. Hooker wannabe.* Like my mama always advises, take a little, give a little.

"Yeah, I'm glad to be here." I took my index fingers and flicked my fourteen-carat gold earrings. "I've already got two holes in my ear. Didn't need a bullet to put another hole in my head. No thanks to you."

We started walking away from the commotion, presumably to avoid the media on the ground. My colleagues were being kept *way back* as usual. When that happens in broadcast news, we rely on choppers. But it was a windy day. That explains it. I figured the TV stations hadn't gotten the choppers up yet to get an aerial view of the bank and everything else that was going on. They might not even know that I was out yet. Or that Zeke, God bless him, was still in.

The S.W.A.T. team had set up a think tank in a coffee shop across the street, at an angle from the bank. They had pushed all the little tables together and there were a couple of portable phones and walkie-talkies lying around.

Wild Bill was standing at the head of the table and everyone else was at the other end, like a class listening to the professor. I made eye contact with one of the "students." Guy's name is Sweeney. He's over six feet, beer-brown hair, slim face, combs his hair slicked back, quick to laugh outside of the job. He's cool with Doug and, like me, the guy's a pro so neither of us acknowledged the other; but our eyes said hello.

In the middle of the room the S.W.A.T. team had set up a big white board. In big blue marker it said "Hostage Situation." Then underneath there were columns.

I walked over to the board and thumped it with my index finger.

"You don't have much info here. I see under SUS-PECTS you've written: 'More than one' with a question mark." I picked up the marker and slashed out all the words EXCEPT the word "one." "One suspect inside." Then I wrote: "Name is Brett." Next Wild Bill had written under WEAPONS: "Gun and a Bomb." In front of the word *gun*, I put the number two. I went under the word HOSTAGES where Wild Bill had drawn a blank line and then written the word *number* next to it. I put the marker on the blank as if I were going to fill it in.

Then I stopped.

"Keep going. We need all the info we can get as fast as we can. That teller who came out before you is such a nervous wreck, she can hardly talk. She's sedated. And I've got questions."

"So have I, Bill. Like where's the tape? I've got to get it on air. Now."

"No. That's not the plan."

"I know it's not YOUR PLAN. It's the plan of the man in the bank toting two guns and a bomb. Why didn't you play the tape? It's stupid to ignore his demands."

Wild Bill thumped the table with his knuckles. "No, what's stupid is letting some perp pull our strings like we're his puppets. Why let every nut in Chicago think all they gotta do is grab some hostages and they're TV material?"

"But this guy Brett is serious. I know you looked at the tape, right?"

"What cop worth his shield wouldn't?"

"Well then. What did ya see, Bill? Huh?"

"I'll tell you what I saw, Georgia. I saw a guy sweating bullets. A guy who is dangerous and stupid. I saw a perp we can take out, easy. That's what I saw."

"Well I saw more, Bill. Eyeball to GUN BARREL. Eyeball to BOMB. Sometimes his eyes were cold and determined. Then other times he didn't look like he knew which way was up. This guy Brett is not stable. I say we play the tape and give him something. Then with a little time we can coax him out."

"And I suppose you want your station to air it first, then you'll make copies and pass 'em out to the other news outlets?"

"Yeah. Doesn't that make the most sense, Bill? Brett says he's going to start shooting hostages if that tape isn't played. He's got a TV from the staff lounge propped up on a desk in front. He's watching for that tape. He's tuned into my station. Just give me the tape and I can get it on ASAP."

"Did you lie to me on the phone, Georgia?"

"Lie about what?"

"About trying to get an exclusive on this thing. Are you trying to pull a fast one?"

"No! I'm trying to keep a paddy wagon from hauling a body bag away from here in less than"—I looked up at the wall clock, 11:10 A.M.—"oh about twenty minutes. Understand? That's how long I've got left to get that tape on air. My TV station is less than five blocks away. I can make it. Just give me the tape!"

Wild Bill crossed his arms. "It's a bad idea, Georgia. If you negotiate with this type of man they just stay longer. Then they wind up killing people. We've got our best snipers up on the roof of this coffee shop. All we need to do is figure a way to get the perp back to the phone."

"We don't have time for that!"

"Yeah we do. WITH YOU. You're the bait."

The only time I liked being called that was when a bartender tossed me and Peaches out of a blues joint AFTER we scammed our way in when we were only sixteen; man said we were the sexiest jailbait he'd ever seen. Flattered then, not flattered now. "Come on Bill. What's the deal?"

"Here's what you can do to save your cameraman and the rest of the hostages, Georgia. Tell this guy on the bullhorn that you're going to call on the phone. He likes you. Trusts you. Phone rings. He answers it. We hit him."

"How can you possibly take a chance like that?"

Wild Bill grabbed a set of plans on the desks. "This development just opened three months ago. The same architect designed the bank. The plans for this place match the bank across the street."

"Same dimensions?"

"To the inch, Georgia. We can pinpoint exactly where the perp'll be when he answers the phone. All we have to do is set the crosshairs up and nail the guy."

"But what about the other hostages?"

"They'll be safe. The bank teller said he locked all the hostages up."

"Not Zeke. Zeke is OUT FRONT with Brett. That's where we made the videotape. And there's the bomb. Did you forget about that?"

"I've seen the tape, Georgia. The bomb is in that sack on the counter behind him. It's not taped to him. We shoot this guy in the head and he won't have time to piss himself let alone get to that bomb and detonate it."

Did Wild Bill think this was some kind of crazy Wild West show and he was the main attraction? Did he think that he was SO SMART and SO HARD AS NAILS that he could take chances with other people's lives? Gamble with other people's loved ones? I looked into Wild Bill's eyes. He had no intention of trying to find Brett's daughter Mandy or negotiating with him either for that matter. Wild Bill wanted a kill. I called him on it.

"Do you *really* want everyone to get out safely?"

"You've got some gall asking me that. I got more than thirty years on the job—"

"No doubt you have skills, commander. All I'm saying is that your plan is aggressive. AND MAYBE, *just maybe,* that has something to do with the fact that the mayor has been kicking the department's butt about being soft on crime, huh? You wouldn't be trying to take this guy out in a blaze of *S.W.A.T.dom* to score points with the mayor and the public. That's not it, huh?"

Wild Bill slammed his knuckles into the table. The papers flew off. The other officers just stood there like statues waiting for this man to blow. But hey, they didn't know that I'm only scared of a few things in life and Wild Bill is not among 'em.

"Georgia . . . I don't like having pissing matches with people who wear panties."

Oh no he didn't fix his mouth to say that.

Wild Bill stomped his feet and stood flat-footed, hands out and pointed at the floor. "Where am I standing, huh Georgia, where?"

I was so mad that I couldn't say a mumbling word even to answer that retarded question. So Wild Bill had to answer it himself.

"I'm standing right here at this table. By myself. You and everybody else are down at the other end. That means I'm top dog in this room. I call all the shots. I have the experience and the guts to get this hostage situation wrapped up. And if that guy's toe has to have a tag on it, then so be it."

"It might not just be him, Bill," I growled. "Did you ever think of that? Somebody else might get hurt or worse?"

"No. Because I don't think in the negative. I'm thinking positive and I'm thinking preventative. I don't want to set up S.W.A.T. teams in coffeehouses all around the city because every guy whose little girl starts running around with some loser suddenly decides it's okay to take hostages and make us fix the problem for 'em.'"

I was speechless. And for me, that's something. Why was he being so rigid? I knew he was a piece of work before, but never did I think that he was as narrow-minded as this. My eyes dropped and then I saw it.

The tape.

I didn't look up because I didn't want my eyeballs to tell Wild Bill what I had in mind. Doug once told me that old-school cops could get to a point where they could tell whether someone was telling the truth or lying—now whether or not they could prove it in court was another thing all together.

When you're a reporter you're part storyteller, part investigator, part actor. My twin sister Peaches and me come from a long line of drama queens too. Our grandmother used to sing on the Negro vaudeville circuit way back in the day. Between her natural talent passed down through the genes PLUS from all the times Peaches would get us in trouble with grandma as kids and we needed to get out of a switching, I'd learned how to cry on cue. So I went to work, baby. When I felt the first tear roll down, I glanced up.

"Okay, Bill. I'm sorry."

"Jesus H. Christ, don't cry."

"I'll do whatever you say. We'll go with your plan." Tears were rolling now. One of the officers handed me a hanky. I took it and blew my nose.

"Get yourself together, Georgia." Wild Bill walked around the table. He took my arm. "Sit down, then let's get this thing done."

I just nodded. The tape was on the corner of the

table, just behind him. "Can I go to the bathroom?" I
walked around him and stepped back. I could feel the
tape against my fingertips. I grabbed it and slipped it
under the jacket wrapped around my waist. "Where's the
bathroom?"

One of the other cops pointed it out. My fingertips
ached holding the tape against the small of my back. I
acted like I was gushing humility as I walked backward.
"I'm sorry, Bill. You're right. I've been holding things up."

"Fine. Fine. Just stop crying and calm down so you
can make the phone call."

I nodded and then he turned around and started
giving orders for the snipers to get into place. I slipped
into the bathroom. My fingertips gave out. The tape fell
to the floor. Did anyone hear it? I quickly picked it up before peeking out the door. All the S.W.A.T. boys were
busy listening to Wild Bill. Man was he going to be mad
when he saw this tape pop up on air. *For real.*

I turned BACK AROUND and checked out the
ladies' room. Like fate, there was a stall right under the
window. I flipped down the lid on the toilet, stepped up,
and opened the window. The ground was too far off for
my liking, but there was a garbage bin under the window. Cups and plates, coffee grounds, empty sour cream
wrappers, and three big cardboard boxes. I shrugged.
THEN I JUMPED.

What? You thought I wouldn't? Hey, I've been trashed before. Talked about too. I remember one time I wound up being the talk of the town back in Ohio, where I landed my first reporting job. Most folks don't know it, but back in the day you paid some *serious* dues to get on the air. In small markets you shot your own video. That meant lugging around a big old bulky camera, tape and lights to boot. ALL THAT for the grand salary of: *about ten thousand dollars*. There were *no Zekes* unless you were going live.

Anyway, there was a big snowstorm one day and I got sent out afterward to do a sort of "making the best of it" piece. I had the luxury of getting a cameraman and truck to go live. We picked this cute little neighborhood with children in the back, making snowmen. Just as the camera started rolling, they decided to go WILD CHILD and have a snowball fight.

One of those snowballs hit me *right in the ear,* ON

CAMERA. Who knew? I wasn't braced for it so my foot slipped and I landed right on my sled. My cameraman caught one right in the *jingle bells*. Now mind you I'm live, right? What did I do? Most reporters would have gotten up and kept talking. I stopped my weather update and made me some snowballs and started *firing two-handed*. I'm no snow bunny or punk either for that matter. I laid all of them out, turned around, and finished my story—LIVE.

I ended up being the "kicker"—that's the *hey this'll make you laugh story*—on every newscast in town that night PLUS got my picture in the local daily the next day. Point made: nothing stops a reporter from getting the story.

So landing in the trash bin is no biggie. I jumped out of that mess as quick as I could and hightailed it to Channel 8. Our studio is near north, by the lakefront. We're in a hip, booming area with costly condos and trendy restaurants and *foo-foo fruit* and veggie shops where ONE apple costs a buck-fifty just because it's organic; *shoot, I don't care if it's biblical and was grown in the Garden of Eden, AH BUCK-FIFTY? Please.*

In all that mucho metrodom, our studio is the last GODZILLA. It's an old two-story building that was once a warehouse. Our network threw in some floors and a brick front and a logo that's a crest with a camera inside—impressive and now as recognizable in news as both the all-seeing CBS eye and the funky fantail of the NBC peacock.

I just wish that INSIDE we had some COLD AIR in the summer and some REAL HEAT in the winter. And since I'm wishing, I wish it wasn't so darn dusty AND that whatever it is that's hanging from the ceiling behind all that ugly pipe overhead would quit falling on my crown and—*well, ya get my drift.*

As much of an eyesore as it is, Channel 8 was a *sight for these hostage eyes* I tell you. I wanted to kiss that skid-marked foyer before I ran from the lobby back to the newsroom.

Fate isn't always fickle. That's 'cause the first person I eyeballed was Clarice, who is a researcher at Channel 8 PLUS my best girlfriend at work. I blurted out the 411 on everything that had happened. Clarice hugged me and said, "Girl, I'm glad you're okay *but Lord you stink.*"

I sniffed as we hustled our way down the long hallway. "Yeah, nobody's going to hire me to do a deodorant commercial anytime soon. That's for sure."

"Hey—you want me to call your mother and tell her you're okay?" Clarice pulled out a Virginia Slim and lit it. "Or do you wanna just wait and call her after you get off air?"

"Mama doesn't have access to a TV at work. She doesn't even know. Thank God."

"Uh-huh—*yeah she does.*"

How? I thought. Then I shoved Clarice. "Big mouth."

"I ain't thinking about you, Georgia. How could I NOT tell her? MY LUCK she'd find out later that I knew and didn't say anything. *Then ooooh weee,* I'd be in trouble." Clarice rolled her eyes and blew smoke in the air. "I like life. You know how your mama is."

We reached the fork in the hallway.

"Clarice, get this tape to the studio crew. Right now." I tossed it to her. "And hurry. The police are on my heels. I'm headed to set."

"Like *that?*" Clarice said as she broke into a trot to get the tape ready to play live.

"In the raw."

Clarice teased. *"Raw is right. You're so funky my eyes are watering."*

I teased her back by kissing my fingertips and smacking my butt.

Clarice responded. "Welcome back, Georgia!"

I sprinted down the other hallway and burst onto the set. Pete was sitting there with the camera, hot to do a cut-in when we got the latest info on the hostage situation.

The crew applauded.

I took a bow. "Thanks for the love."

Pete asked, "Where's Zeke?"

"In jeopardy."

I hopped up on the set. A studio technician began to mike me up just as the makeup artist ran over with powder and brush in one hand. She took one look at my messed-up mug and froze.

I borrowed a line from Reverend Jesse Jackson. "Keep hope alive." She combed my hair back and touched up my makeup as best she could.

The producer was sitting with the director and the other staff members in an out-of-sight booth filled with equipment and monitors.

"Soon to be hot, folks," the floor director shouted.

The floor director, who takes cues from the director

and passes them on to the on-air talent, barked, "Tape is cued."

I checked the digital clock that reads time down to the frames. One minute. Thirty seconds. Eight frames.

I was sweating. "Let's roll y'all. C'mon."

The floor director stood in front of the middle camera. "Coming out in one minute."

Pete panicked. "I don't have any copy."

"Wing it."

"Wing it?" he balked.

"Thirty seconds!"

"Yeah Pete. Give and go baby. Just say we've got the latest on the story. And toss it to me, kiddo."

"Ten to you Pete."

He straightened up in his seat and draped a serious look across his face. When the camera light went on, and the floor director snapped his fingers, we were live. The graphic that said SPECIAL REPORT flashed on the screen, then dissolved to the set.

Pete:

"Good afternoon, everyone. We have a new development in an ongoing story. A man is holding hostages at Lake Michigan Bank. One of the hostages was our own Georgia Barnett. She joins me now on set with the latest. Georgia?"

I take the toss from him on a camera shot of the both of us. I say thanks before turning into a side camera that's focused only on me.

It's a difficult story to tell. Reporters gather facts

and present them. We are NOT SUPPOSED to inject our-selves into the story. BUT this time I'm part of the story by no choice of my own. My cameraman and I were in Lake Michigan Bank when a gunman burst in carrying a bomb. We thought he would rob the bank, then leave. In-stead he stayed. He says he has a mission. He allowed me to leave with a tape that he wants the police, the press, and you, the public, to see.

Then I looked down. The director rolled the videotape Brett made earlier. From the safety of the anchor desk, I watched Brett's passionate plea. Boy was crazy, but even I got a little misty at his last words:

And to my little girl, if you're out there watching. Daddy is going to fix it, baby. Don't worry. I'll fix it.

Dump tape back to me on set for live Q&A.

"This is a passionate plea for help. Anyone with in-formation about Mandy or the man she is believed to be with—the man on the police alert—please contact your local police department. Lives depend on it. And to the gunman in the bank: we played the tape just like you asked. Don't do anything you'll regret. The police are searching for the couple and I'll do all I can to help find them too. Pete?"

"Georgia, what was it like inside the bank? Did the gunman say anything besides what we heard on tape?"

"Pete, this is a dangerous, ongoing situation. I can-not comment more at this time. I will say, however, that the gunman is afraid for his daughter's safety. BUT he did promise to release EVERYONE unharmed when she turns up safe."

"Thank you, Georgia."

Pete turned back into camera two for a solo shot.

Next we have Tim McNamara live near the scene. Tim is joined by one of the store owners whose business had to be evacuated. Tim?

I was about to leave the set when Clarice's voice came over my earpiece. "Georgia, don't move. Just look at the monitor like you're watching the live interview."

Clarice's gritty voice sounded heavy as stone. Sistah was *way serious.* I did like she asked.

"Cool. Now use your peripheral vision and glance at the studio door—right through that little glass square where folks peek in. There. See 'em? Those are two cops. See 'em?"

I cut my eyes a smidgen and could see their caps and their light blue shirts and the tips of their tin badges. I nodded my head like I was really into the live report. But Clarice knew. The nod was for her.

"They're here for you, girl."

Wild Bill sent them. Had to. He wants them to drag me back to the coffee shop so I can make that call to Brett so they can take him out. *I smiled mischievously.* NO WAY.

"They wanna arrest you."

WHAT!!?

"We told them they had to wait 'til we were off air

because nobody wanted a scene on live TV. They think that door is the only way IN and OUT of the studio. Give me a second. I'm sending an intern wearing a short skirt in. She'll drop an armload of tapes to distract them. Then you know how to sneak out, right? And where to meet me?"

I nodded. The cops were there waiting, watching. After a few seconds I saw them turn and look down. That's when I slid out of the chair and walked through the back of the set. Only the people who worked there knew that there was a back door through the fake Chicago skyline. It led to the loading dock.

I slipped out and ran. I saw Clarice standing on the ramp.

"Arrest me for what?"

"Something about obstruction of justice for taking that tape . . ."

"Say what? Aww. I really got Wild Bill's BVDs in a bunch." I sucked wind. "But those charges are bogus, Clarice. They'll never stick."

Clarice bucked her eyes. "You wanna find out?"

Right. "Okay Clarice, it's clear the cops aren't gonna half-cooperate. I'm going to have to try and find Mandy myself."

"Not all by yourself girl." Then Clarice hit the button that opened the loading dock door. One of our big old white news vans was parked there with the motor still running. Standing next to the van happened to be *three sights for sore eyes.* It was the Video Cowboys. These were the guys that Zeke was supposed to meet at the bar.

I nodded at the van. "Thought all of those oldies but goodies had been retired."

The Video Cowboys said, "We're ALL coming out of retirement today."

A bold smile spread across my face. I was grinning 'cause I knew I would soon be winning.

Who needs the Chicago P.D. or the cavalry for that matter when you've got the Video Cowboys?

Vicente Ochoa—Choke. He was grinning while leaning his 5'6" frame on the van. Choke is ruggedly handsome. He's got dance fever. He'll break out in a salsa strut in a minute.

Right next to him was Paulie, arms folded across his massive chest. He was almost as wide as the van and just as tall. He had on a dark blue cotton sweat suit, Nikes, and a Chicago Bulls cap.

Gunner was standing off to the side. His flat, plank-like body looked like a stake driven into the ground. His black muscle shirt showed off a tattoo on his forearm: *a roaring tiger with its claw up pawing at a helicopter spraying bullets.* His shiny bald head picked up a hint of yellow from the sun and he was chewing the hell out of some gum.

Choke spoke first.

"Hey chica. Heard Zeke's in trouble. We thought you might need some help."

"Do I ever. But I don't know where to start."

"I do." Gunner grunted. He always spoke low and ended his thoughts with questions. "You ready to ride?"

We jumped in the van and eased out of the driveway. I watched the garage door slowly close. About five seconds before the metal edge of the door met the concrete I saw the familiar black lace-ups that most street cops on the Chicago P.D. wear.

Paulie was driving. Paulie taught Zeke how to drive a news van. Does the jury need any more evidence? That means Paulie doesn't give a care WHAT the speedometer reads AND THAT ALSO MEANS I have to HOLD ON for dear life.

Paulie and Gunner were sitting in the front. Choke and I were sitting in the rear on two side seats that faced each other. The rest of the station's Minicam trucks had been updated with digital equipment but we were in an old-school unit with beta equipment. Like the Video Cowboys, it was still good and could get the job done— we could set up a signal and go live from anywhere in the city.

We hit the expressway that runs along the city's fabulous lakefront. The buildings cut clean lines against the pale blue sky. The edgy, contemporary architecture somehow seemed neighborly with the *porch-sitting designs* of the metropolitan skyline. We were passing Grant Park, the lush-plush oasis of speckled landscaping that borders downtown. I glanced at the spurting mist that clung like perspiration to the concrete brow of Buckingham Fountain.

We were heading south. I asked the Video Cowboys, "Where to?"

Paulie answered me. "The Hackman Center in Alsip."

"The Hackman Center? Don't believe I know it."

Choke shrugged, "I kinda do, Georgia." He pulled out a package of Chiclets gum, shaking the box. *"Doggone her time that Clarice.* She's got me jonesin' for a cigarette. Lord I wish I hadn't smelled those smokes! I'm trying SO HARD to kick." He shook most of the gum into his mouth and garbled. "Hackman Center is a nonprofit hospital for veterans."

Paulie gave a sharp laugh. "That's one of the alleged perks of serving your country. A small hospital stuck out in suburban nowhere. The government cut back on funds and that place is a bigger mess than a baby eating with its fingers. Not to mention there's not enough beds. Plus nothing but a bunch of student nurses who can hardly find a guy's butt with a bedpan. It's a dirty shame if you asked me. The vets DESERVE TOP-NOTCH. This other stuff . . . *forget about it.*"

Gunner didn't say a word but once Paulie mentioned veterans, I knew Gunner had to have some kind of a connection with this clue.

"You know the place, Gunner?"

"Yeah. When I saw the video I recognized that laundry bag on the counter. Black bag. Red writing. Then I saw that sweatshirt the guy was wearing. It looked familiar too. I've seen both of them out at Hackman. Do you think the guy is all there?"

Without saying so, Gunner was letting me know that Hackman's a psychiatric facility. Now things were making sense. I started voicing my thoughts. Usually I don't do that, talk out loud, and blurt out what I'm turning over in my head. I like to keep my figuring to myself. But these guys I could trust. They love Zeke just as much as I do. And with Doug out of the country and the cops pissed off at me, the Video Cowboys were becoming the beat of my heart. I told them about the atmosphere inside the bank, focusing on Brett the gunman.

"The guy had some vicious mood swings. Plus a couple of times he said some things that showed me he was struggling."

"Struggling?" Paulie questioned. "Like what?"

"Like he couldn't remember details about his own daughter, Paulie. He wouldn't give up the wanted poster of the mope that his daughter is hanging with because he said he didn't want to forget what the guy looked like."

Choke raised an eyebrow. "That's what you saw in the bank, huh? Now let me put THAT with what I SAW on the tape. He seems like he's overly possessive. *My little chica, poppy's going to fix it.* You know? Stuff like that. He sounded too possessive and too dangerous."

Paulie rammed the accelerator down, cracked a yellow light, and turned the corner, knocking over a wire wastebasket.

"Excuse me," I teased sarcastically. "You missed that little old lady in the wheelchair. That was at least one hundred bonus points, Paulie."

"Good, Georgia. You're breaking my balls just like Zeke would if he were here. I like that."

"I'm worried for him y'all."

Their silence told me they were worried for Zeke too. I settled back for what would be a fifteen-minute drive. It was around noon. I borrowed Choke's cell phone and called Doug in Mexico.

I just wanted to hear his voice and let him know what was going on back here at home. Boyfriend was NOT happy.

"What? You were a hostage? Hang on."

I did. It doesn't take much to get old Doug's juices going; he's hot-blooded in more ways than one, *if ya know what a sister means.* This time though, with the tripped-out news I was laying on him, Doug had every good reason *to percolate.*

"Now. I'm somewhere we can talk, baby. What happened?"

I briefed Doug and listened as my voice graveled and rose, then sunk to a whisper. I guess I had been more afraid than I thought. But it was no time to get weak 'bout the knees. I had a job to do: cover this story and get Zeke and the rest of those hostages out of there safe and sound.

"Watch Wild Bill, baby. You crossed him. And you should have. He was grandstanding as usual. He can't halfway help it though. Early in his career I heard he was too soft on a high-profile case and ever since then he's always putting on this tough-guy, bulldog, *ain't taking no Saddam sons prisoners* type of 'tude whether the situation calls for it or not."

"Meaning?"

"Meaning he'll step on anybody's toes, including pretty ones in a pair of pumps like yours."

"Okay, Doug."

"His right hand is a cat named Carey. They went to high school together. He's tough as hell but I hear he's decent, you know, fair. If he's around, play to him."

"Got it, Doug."

"You're dealing with a lot. It's killing me that I'm away at a time when you need me the most, Georgia. But I gotta wait for the last of the paperwork to get this guy out of the country and back to Chicago." Doug took a long breath. "Maybe I can let my partner handle it solo."

"Doug, that case is the talk of the STATE . . . You can't just skip out on a high-profile assignment like that. Are you kidding me? That guy's been hiding out for two years now; if something goes wrong with the extradition, they'll blame you. AND EVEN IF YOU COULD RUSH IT, you can't hurry an airplane and get here before Brett's deadline. He wants his daughter outside that bank before nightfall and only God can help us find her now." Doug's presence would bring me some peace of mind, *for sure,* but running out on THE JOB was a lose-lose situation.

"You're right, baby. But look, I know you. You'll do all you can do—but remember to be careful. I know you got Zeke's boys with you and Chicago's finest is on the case too. But I'm STILL gonna page my guys and tell them to be at your beck and call. You got Ricky and Bone's numbers, right?"

"You made me memorize them, remember?"

"Yeah, in case of emergency. So if you need their help call 'em. Be careful and be smart. And keep me posted, okay?"

"Okay, bye baby. Be safe, Doug."

"I'm built for this." Doug's tough-guy voice turned soft. "You watch out for you, girl."

I hung up the phone and tried to keep Doug's words in my head: *be careful and be smart*. My mind was kicking into high gear as we turned down the road that led to the veterans' facility.

The Hackman Center was shoved up next to an industrial park in south suburban Alsip. Goethe said architecture is frozen music. If true, then the Hackman Center is an icy blues ballad. It's a cold, sad-looking structure. The white façade of the front is grimy and streaked from the harsh Chicago weather: snowy winters, rainy springs, blistering summers, and frigid falls. Two corner columns of chipped stone were sentry to the long set of steps that led up to the arched double doorway.

There's a parking lot that was added less than ten years ago. It's divided into staff and visitors' spaces. Today the staff spaces only had a few cars. We were the only vehicle in the visitors' section. Gunner led the way while Choke trailed behind us, hoisting the camera on his shoulder to videotape the exterior of the center. That's what we call B-roll . . . or background video, the scene setters.

Once inside we went straight to the hospital's administrative office. Hackman had a director named Charles Lackney. As soon as the secretary saw us, she picked up the phone and hit a button. Two seconds later the director's door flew open.

"Excuse me," Lackney barked. He was a tall man with slouchy posture, tiny, blinky gray eyes, and thick curly hair. "You don't belong here. There will be no filming or interviews here on the grounds."

Hard sell, I thought. "Mr. Lackney, let me explain. I'm Georgia Barnett—"

"With Channel 8 News," he finished my sentence sarcastically. "No media. The last time the media was here, the old director got fired because of some bogus report about mismanagement of funds. That's not happening to me."

"We're not here for that." I explained. "This is urgent."

"Please leave!"

Paulie jumped in. "If we wanted to pull commando journalism on this joint, we would've come in here lights on, cameras blazing." Paulie pointed at Choke. "You see my friend here has the camera down to his side and off. Hear the lady out."

Mr. Lackney pushed forward. "Out!"

Paulie pushed back, "IN! IN!" backing the man into his office. We followed. "Leave the door open so the secretary can see that we ain't filming and Charlie boy here is all in one piece." Paulie pushed him toward the desk. "Sit down and listen to the lady."

Mr. Lackney plopped down in his chair, his face cherry red with anger. I love my Paulie. He's *Terminator tough,* baby. I got down to business. "Did you hear about the hostage situation at Lake Michigan Bank?"

"No."

I turned around and glanced at a wall unit full of books and files. There was a television in the middle and a small radio on his desk. Both were off.

Choke said, "Well, one of your patients is the gun-man."

"One of my patients? That's impossible. We don't have outpatients here. All of our patients are committed and we give them the best of care around the clock."

Paulie burst out, "PLEASE. *The hallway is filthy and the air smells like urine.*"

I cut my eyes at him. *We're trying to get this man's help. Don't make him mad.* Paulie got my drift and I went back to Lackney. "Look—he could be one of your former patients. He told me his name is Brett. He's a small-built man and—"

"Sorry, I don't know anybody by that name and besides I can't give out any information about our patients. That's the rule."

"Break it, *esse.*" Choke turned on the TV. "Might keep somebody from getting killed. Take a look at the news." My competition was on. Channel 8 had shared the wealth and gotten dubs of Brett's public plea to the other news outlets.

Gunner pointed out the details as tape rolled. "That sweatshirt I've seen around here. And that laundry bag too. THAT IS the Hackman logo, isn't it?"

He nodded. "How do you know so much, Mr., uh . . ."

"Gunner. Vietnam vet. Had a couple of buddies in here I used to visit. Do you know this guy?"

By the look on his face you could tell that he did.

Gunner growled, "Is it going to kill you to tell us his name?"

"Brett Andronte." But next out of his mouth was the

administration's party line: "But I can't divulge ANY personal information about the patients here. I shouldn't have even told you his name."

As soon as he said that, two hulking orderlies filled the doorway. Lackney acted like a punk whose big brothers had just arrived. *Now boyfriend got big and brave.* "FINALLY," he huffed, looking at the orderlies. Then he focused his *big and bad act on us.* "Yeah, so like I said. No filming and no interview. OUT. Mike. Larry. Take them out through the back way. Now!"

The Video Cowboys looked at the orderlies in the doorway and didn't move an inch. I mean, *they didn't wiggle a toe in their Timberlands.*

So I stepped up. "Let's go guys."

They looked at me like I had a jack-in-the-box on my shoulders and the clown had just popped out.

"C'mon. We're beat." And I started walking. Paulie caught up with me and whispered, "You gotta be kidding."

"Not yet," I whispered back.

"When yet?" he grumped back in a low voice. "Time is ticking away."

We left single file and the orderlies walked us toward a rear exit; we were in front, the orderlies behind us. I noticed a laundry room door coming up, and outside it in the hall was a big cotton bin on wheels filled with sheets.

I nudged Paulie with my elbow and nodded toward the bin. Then I whispered, "Yet."

As soon as the Video Cowboys and I cleared that bin, Paulie grabbed it by the corner and flung it around right into the knees of the two orderlies. They doubled over. One of them flopped and then threw a wild punch at Paulie.

Paulie ducked and fired back, connecting with a right cross to the jaw. The other guy grabbed Paulie by the wrist and flung him into the wall.

My man Choke and Gunner were standing there watching like it was the Friday Night Fights on cable.

I shouted at them, "Help Paulie!"

Choke laughed, "But there's only two of them." He nudged Gunner. "*Cinco dólares* says neither one of them lays a punch on Paulie."

"Five bucks?" Gunner thumbed his nose. "Paulie's got it covered for sure. But a shutout? Nah, you forget about age, my friend. What makes you think Paulie's still as good as he used to be?"

The two orderlies now had Paulie by the arms. Paulie kicked one in the shin. When he let go, Paulie punched the other orderly in the oven. He slumped to the floor. Paulie ducked two quick punches by the orderly still standing before taking him out with a hard left jab that landed right on the curve of the chin.

What did I hear next? *Fingers snapping a cha-cha beat.* Choke was over there doing a salsa step. "My man's still got it." Choke whipped around, then began snapping the fingers of his left hand near his ear but reaching out his right hand, palm up. Gunner pulled out a bill and slapped it in Choke's hand.

"I get a taste!" Paulie huffed. "Age my butt."

"Come on you guys!" I shrugged. "Now what?"

"*This what,*" Gunner said. "Don't you know I've always got a backup plan?"

Choke asked, "What about these *putos?*"

Paulie grabbed a sheet and began to rip it up. He tied up the orderlies and gagged them. "I won't make it too tight. With *some real effort* they'll be able to wiggle their way out after they come to. So let's get rolling, Gunner. What's the plan?"

Gunner's plan landed us outside. We found ourselves in the storage shack on the edge of the complex, about ten yards away from the parking lot. Gunner made a quick call on his cell phone and told us we were waiting for someone named Hap.

Gunner filled us in. "Some of the employees come back here and smoke. Funky-looking, ain't it?"

"Yeah. And why so far?" I asked. "They could just stand outside the main building."

Gunner deadpanned, "Didn't say what they were smoking, did I?"

The door cracked open and a small-built African-American man stepped in. He had on a white uniform, white cap, and an apron stained with food. He wiped his hands on the apron and nodded at all of us. "I'm Hap."

Gunner shook his hand. "Thanks for coming man. Did you get it?"

Hap looked around. "Too many ears."

"These people are my ears, my eyes, my heart. Nothing they can't see or hear and nothing I can't trust them with. Did you get it?"

Hap didn't blink.

"Me and Hap got to be real cool when I was visiting one of my friends here. He took extra good care of my buddy and I took care of his niece. She needed some money for books. Kid's in med school." Gunner pulled out a money clip. "Come on, Hap. I gave you the name.

Your nurse friend was able to get a copy of the file from the ward, wasn't she?"

Hap still didn't come across.

I pushed him. "Hap, we're not here to get you into trouble. We've got a friend who's being held hostage with a lot of other innocent folk by a man who was a patient here. If he kills somebody, can your conscience take it KNOWING you could have helped?"

Hap nodded. Then he pulled out a thin medical file he had doubled over and stuffed in the small of his back. He squeezed it like Mr. Whipple squeezed Charmin on the TV commercial.

Gunner prodded him this time. "C'mon, man. You think I want trouble for you or for me? We tried to get this file the right way, by going through Lackney. Think it did any good?"

Paulie jumped in. "He was a knucklehead about it."

Gunner finished talking. "I only had you on standby, Hap, IF and ONLY IF everything else failed. We've been helping each other for a long time. Would I jam you up?"

"Guess not." Hap held out the file.

Gunner reached for it. I stayed his hand. I told the Video Cowboys, "This is it, no turning back. If we take this file it's like stealing government property."

"You're right," Gunner said. "Now answer me this. Do you think we could POSSIBLY get in any more trouble than we're ALREADY IN?"

Paulie sucked wind. "And if so, do we give ah care?" Then he grabbed the file. We cut out of there, got in the van, drove a few blocks, and stopped to check out the new info we had just scammed.

It read:

Brett Andronte, 57 years old.
Admitted: May 2003.
Came from the Brentwood facility.

The notes said that Brett had served in 'Nam for three years in a unit that specialized in explosives—making and detonating bombs.

I told the Video Cowboys, "That's NOT good news. Brett knows what he's doing." They agreed.

The file continued:

Brett has a brain disorder that affects his
hippocampus—he forgets things, and sometimes re-
experiences tragic memories without warning.

Paulie asked, "What's a hippocampus? Sounds like something you'd find at the zoo."

We laughed, then I schooled them. *"Hippocampus* is Greek for sea horse. In psychological terms, it's the part of the brain that's responsible for our emotional memory bank."

Gunner seemed surprised. "Where'd you learn all that?"

"Last year when the mental health convention came to town. Olivia was out on maternity leave, so I covered the medical beat for a while. Good thing we snatched this file. Now some things are making sense."

"Like what, chica?"

"Like why he held on to that police sketch, Choke. Remember I told you we had to shoot it on camera because Brett wouldn't send it out, said he needed it to remember. And then when I asked for more details about his daughter Mandy, he got all mad and confused?"

"Yeah," Gunner jumped in. "Now we know why." Gunner flipped through the file and came to a page with a picture stapled to it.

I looked hard. It took a second to pick out Brett. And then I spotted him looking at ease, sharing a laugh with some of the other patients. "He looks good here, huh, Gunner?"

"My buddy said they would give out rewards sometimes to people who were making progress, who were doing good. Take them on outings, like baseball games. He must have been doing well when this picture was taken. I wonder what made him snap?"

Paulie stitched his fingers and popped his knuckles. "Worrying about your kid will make you snap. Speaking of . . . what's it say in there about his daughter, anything?"

We shuffled through the papers. I noticed that half of them came from the photocopied letterhead of another facility. The paperwork indicated that at one time he had been at a private facility, until the money ran out, that is. Under the next of kin it listed his daughter, Mandy Mitchell . . . age 25 . . . and an address.

Paulie cranked the engine. "We're there."

"Aye," Choke said. "Not the same last name. Must be a love child."

"Or," I said, "she could be married to that slob on the police alert. Maybe he's an abusive husband."

Paulie growled, "Better not be. I can't stand a guy that puts a beating on a woman. I've got nieces this

Mandy kid's age. When we find Mandy, I'm gonna ask her if this guy is putting a beating on her. If he is, I'll personally tear him apart. I'll lay that chump out like a dead man right on that apartment floor."

But who knew?

There was already one there.

Who ever gets used to seeing a dead body? Cops? Maybe. Soldiers? Maybe. Big-city TV reporters? Not me.

We kept our radio tuned into WGN to catch all the latest on the hostage situation. All reports said it remained at a standstill. No word out from Brett. And the cops hadn't made a move on the bank.

I knew it was just a matter of time. And that time was truly a-wasting. *But not on our account.* We were humping. Jamming our way to the address in the file for Mandy. It was half a city away on the north side.

"Base to Video Cowboys. Come in Cowboys."

That was Clarice calling us over the two-way radio. Other TV news trucks can pick up the two-way frequency so you always have to be careful what you say. You also had to consider that I was a fugitive so Clarice couldn't use my name at all.

Gunner picked up the radio. "Cowboys here. What's cracking, Clarice?"

"Just wanted to get a handle on your progress."

"We got what we needed from the center and now we're on our way to the next location. Looks good. Roger that?"

"Okay. Keep me posted. Gunner, tell your crew ONE OF THEM needs to call their mama before we BOTH get killed. Base out."

All the Video Cowboys roared with laughter.

"Chica, I thought I had *mama drama* with my mother always taking my ex's side. They fuss at me about spoiling my daughter. She's sixteen and keeps my pockets turned inside out."

I reached out my hand. "Well my mama's gonna turn me inside out for not making this call sooner. Let me use your cell. Mine's still on the floor back at the bank where Brett made all of us dump out our purses and wallets."

I rang up my mother. She turned into Mother Teresa.

"Bless my child, Lord. Are you okay, baby?"

"I'm okay, Mama. Just anxious with Zeke still in there and all. We're working on getting him out and everybody else too, hopefully."

"You know I'm praying for him. Georgia, honey, you should make an appointment to see a doctor."

"Why? I'm okay, Ma."

The saint act turned with a roar. "WELL, YOU WON'T BE *after I get ahold of Miss-I-ain't-got-enough-sense-to-call-my-mama.*"

"Maaaah . . . *Not now.*"

"I can't believe you DIDN'T EVEN call me and let me know you were okay! Thank goodness for Clarice. Now that child is thoughtful."

"CHICKEN is what she is."

"Excuse me?"

"Nothing Mama. Listen, I gotta go. When this is all over I'll give you the scoop—I'm with friends so don't worry and please understand."

"And you understand something too."

"What?"

"I love you."

She made me smile. "Back 'atcha old girl." Mama always gave me and Peaches drama, but she kept me grounded. But soon I would have to deal with a different kind of drama. THAT drama would jump off at Mandy's apartment.

We arrived at her building just as I wrapped up my call. It was one of those multiunit deals, all brick, well kept, in a working-class neighborhood. Streets clean. Pretty quiet. Mandy's apartment was on the first floor rear. When we didn't get an answer at her apartment, we rang the super.

A stocky man in grimy jeans and a paint-stained shirt came to the door. He was holding a brush in his hand. His mustache twitched as he squinted at us through the glass pane of the door.

He sized up Choke. "Who you look for, *hombre?*"

Choke began rattling off words in Spanish. They had a lengthy exchange. The rest of us just stood there waiting. The man nodded and opened the door and began walking us down the hallway to the stairs. I needed to be clued in.

"What did he say, Choke?"

"I told him who we were and why we were looking for Mandy. Orlando said he heard about the hostage situation on the radio while he was painting a vacant apartment. He doesn't know where she worked but said he would let us in the apartment to see if we could find something to help track her down."

When we got to Mandy's apartment, the super didn't have to let us in. The door was open and you could see that the apartment had been tossed.

The super said something in Spanish.

We looked at Choke. He translated. *"There goes her security deposit."*

I rolled my eyes and Choke shrugged, hefted the camera on his shoulder, and began shooting video of the scene.

When we cleared the doorway, we could see BLOOD on the hardwood floors.

I told the Video Cowboys, "Don't touch anything with your bare hands."

Paulie warned, "Yeah. Go easy guys."

Then he led the way. Everything that wasn't nailed down was broken. Chairs. Cocktail tables. Glass. The mirror on the wall. I saw a picture still on the mantle. I picked it up with the hanky that Zeke had given me. It was a photo of a young woman around Mandy's age; she resembled Brett around the eyes and had a similar boxed jaw. To be sure I asked the super, "Mandy?"

"Sí."

I pointed to the man in the photo. "Choke—ask him if that's her husband or her boyfriend."

Choke spoke to the super. He translated back. "That's her boyfriend. Says he moved in here about a month ago. He never liked him because there seemed to be something sneaky about him."

Paulie asked, "What's his name?"

The super answered, "Herc."

A burst of sunlight coming through the window in the bedroom grabbed my attention. That sunbeam fell DIRECTLY on a set of ankles; pale ankles that were twisted awkwardly. As I walked around to get a better view, I had to stifle a scream. I knelt near the body that was face down.

"A lot of blood," I said.

"Mucho," Choke said over my shoulder.

Gunner walked around me. He grabbed a pillow off the bed and took the case and wrapped it around his hand like a big kitchen mitten. Then he turned the body over.

I looked at the photo from the mantle. I visualized the sketch on the police alert.

Choke conferred with the super and told us, "It ain't Herc. The super says he doesn't know who this guy is. He's never seen him before, Georgia."

"Wonder who he is?"

Paulie shrugged, "Cops'll have to figure that out."

Choke advised the super to call the police while we went through some papers Mandy had tucked away in a little office space she had created out of an extra closet.

What did we find?

I'd make it all clear in my live report. You see I knew that I was supposed to communicate with Brett by TV. With the cops on the way to the apartment, we left to set up a live shot in the neighborhood. Close to the scene but with no identifiable streets. We didn't want the cops to catch us since I was still wanted on that bogus warrant that Wild Bill Whelk had put out on me.

Now, the Video Cowboys and I KNEW that the

competition would be reporting that the body of a dead man was found in that apartment. Wouldn't take long for the cops to put two and two together and figure out who the apartment was rented to and her connection to the hostage situation.

Brett needed to know three things. One: that we knew who he was. Two: that the dead man in the apartment was NOT his daughter's boyfriend and BOTH OF THEM were still out there somewhere. And three: we were WORKING HARD to find them.

Choke had shot all the video that we needed. Gunner edited together the material. And now Paulie had powered up the truck, raised the antenna, and was enabling me to go live. It was 2 P.M.

I had my earpiece in and was talking to the producer back at the station. A monitor at my feet showed me our air. I saw the SPECIAL REPORT graphic fill the screen as we cut into programming.

It was time to get ready. Opening my notepad, I went to where I'd written a script to go with the video we had shot and edited together. I was going to voice it over right from the field.

The director cued me and the camera was hot. Hundreds of thousands of viewers were watching me live. But I wasn't thinking about them. This was for Brett. This was for Zeke.

Good afternoon everyone. I'm Georgia Barnett. I'm live on the north side with an update on the search for Mandy, the daughter of the gunman holding hostages at Lake Michigan Bank.

The director rolled the videotape that the Video Cowboys had shot and edited. The first shot was of a photo of Brett that was in his file from the Hackman Center.

The gunman has been identified as fifty-seven-year-old Brett Andronte. He is a decorated Vietnam vet. His military records list him as an explosives expert. After the war, Andronte held several jobs, the last one, seven years ago as a mechanic.

The next shots were of the Hackman Center.

He is currently a patient at the Hackman Center in Alsip. He was transferred there one year ago from a private facility in Evanston.

The next shot was of the photo of Mandy and her boyfriend that I found in the apartment. It started tight on Mandy then slowly pulled to include Herc.

Andronte's daughter is Mandy Mitchell, age twenty-five. She was married for one year then divorced.

Shot now includes Herc.

Residents in the building where she lives ID this man as her current boyfriend—Herc—his last name and age unknown.

Cut to file video of Brett in the bank holding up the police sketch.

Herc IS a dead ringer for the suspect shown in the police sketch held up by Brett Andronte.

Cut to video of the doorway and blood in the ramshackle apartment.

BUT HE IS NOT, repeat, NOT the man found murdered in Mandy's apartment earlier this afternoon. That victim has not been identified. The coroner's office will perform an autopsy to determine the exact cause of death.

Dump tape back to me live.

To Brett inside the bank: we are still looking for your daughter and her boyfriend, Herc. There were no signs in the apartment that SHE was hurt. In fact, her suitcase and some of her clothes were gone. This might indicate that she planned to run. Every effort is being made to find your daughter. To the viewing audience: take a look at the photo now on the screen . . . If you have seen either Mandy or Herc . . . please call police. Do not approach them. They may be armed and dangerous. I'm Georgia Barnett, reporting live back to you in the newsroom.

I stood still as stone until we were cleared.

Paulie smiled at me from behind the camera. "Good job. That's old-school reporting. Now . . . where to, Georgia?"

To the place that I conveniently LEFT out of my report—Mandy's job. She worked as a flight attendant at Midway Airport for a start-up company called Red Eye Airlines.

We had to take two expressways to get there but with Paulie driving like he had the devil on his back, we made it in twenty-five minutes.

I left Mandy's place of business OUT OF MY RE-PORT because I didn't want to put the competition on her trail. They would only want to scoop. I wanted to find Mandy to make sure she got to that bank. That was the only way that Zeke and the other hostages would get out alive.

If there's one thing I've learned as an adult, it's that where you work dramatically impacts your life. That's true, in part, because co-workers are *nosy as hell*. They check out the kind of car you drive, want to know where you live so they can figure out how much bank ya got, and they EVEN like to check out the cuddle pictures on your desk. Don't matter y'all if they're of your sweetheart, yo' mama, or your dog. Co-workers are just nosy.

And no matter how much of a private dancer you THINK you are, SOMEBODY at the J-O-B is trying to cut in.

One of Mandy's co-workers told us, "She got fired about three days ago. Took it hard."

Another co-worker countered, "Thought she quit. That's what I heard."

The Video Cowboys and I were at the ticket counter for Red Eye Airlines. Skip H.R. I needed the *skinny* without the *fat bureaucracy*. Choke was shooting passenger video. Gunner, Paulie, and I had stopped a couple of flight attendants who were waiting to fly out.

"She always acted funny, you know?" one of her co-workers said. "I flew with her to Mexico a couple of times. Mandy always seemed antsy, maybe *bitchy* is a better word."

Another flight attendant weighed in, "Maybe it's because her father's been so sick. She would always work as much as she could to get money to keep him in that expensive hospital. Brentwood. Out in Evanston."

"Not anymore," I told them. "He was in another facility." *Huh, the funky economy must have cut Mandy's purse strings.* I asked, "What do you know about her boyfriend, Herc?" I showed them the picture. "Did she talk about him? Where did they like to go hang out?"

"Nice picture," one co-worker said, holding the photo before handing it back to me. "Never mentioned him to me."

The other flight attendant knew more. "I saw him with her a couple of times. They looked pretty natural

together, maybe a little intense. But I'll tell you who'd
know better. A guy named Steve Watson, works in remote parking, drives the employee shuttle from there to
here. He's a sweetheart; has two cute kids. I'm pretty
sure he's tight with Herc; that's how he got the job."

The Video Cowboys and I checked with the route
supervisor. He said that this guy Steve was starting his
shift and was over at the garage checking out his vehicle.

We got there and one of the other drivers waved us
toward a checkpoint area out back where drivers could
wash, gas up, and put air in the tires.

Paulie was in front of the Video Cowboys, leading
the way. I was trailing behind, using Gunner's cell to call
Clarice to see if the competition had made any headway
on the story.

I heard Paulie call out, "Hey Steve. Steve Watson."

A guy's head popped up in the bus closest to us. He
walked to the front, stepped off the bus, and stopped in
front of us. He was a small man, curly dark brown hair.
Average features except for a rugged chin and a dimpled
smile. "Can I help you?"

"Georgia Barnett, Channel 8 News." I pointed to the
Video Cowboys. "And this is my crew. We want to ask
you some questions about Herc and Mandy."

Steve's smile turned downward. "They in trouble?"

I told him, "We're not the police. So we're not trying
to jam them up. But we need Mandy. Her father has
taken a bunch of hostages at a bank and he's threatening
to kill them UNLESS we find his daughter and bring her
to him."

Steve shook his head. "I don't know where they are.
And I don't like having this conversation."

"Well, you're friends, right? Where did Herc and Mandy like to hang out?"

Steve just shrugged. You could tell that he was holding back. All of us could. "Sorry." He turned around to get back on the bus.

"Wait," Paulie grabbed him. "Who said the conversation was over?"

Whoever started shooting at us, THAT'S WHO. Bullets started flying.

A shot crackled just over Paulie's head. The glass in the bus window shattered. We all ran for cover in the interior of the vehicle.

Another bullet careened off the door, tearing off the rubber molding near Choke's shoulder. I was the last one to make it in.

Another shot whizzed by my heel as I finally cleared the doorway.

We all hunkered down.

"Somebody wants you guys to back off," Steve bellowed. *He was a real master of the obvious.*

"Forget about it," Paulie said. "We're not backing off an inch."

Two more bullets came tearing into the bus.

I figured out the shooting pattern. "The shots are coming from the left flank, by the bushes over there. We're sitting ducks where we are."

Gunner asked if Steve could slide to the front and drive us out of here but he hissed out a long no and covered his head.

Gunner began crawling on his hands and knees toward the front of the bus.

Oh God, I thought. "Be careful, Gunner."

"I was in 'Nam, remember?"

The next bullet came tearing through the window. Still Gunner tried to get into the chair. Another bullet ricocheted off the front fender.

Choke shouted for Gunner to hurry up, "*¡Apúrate! ¡Apúrate!*"

Another bullet hit the ground. We heard it crackle against the concrete. That was Gunner's cue.

He hopped into the chair, cranked the engine, and floored it. The bus lurched forward, ramming into the side of the chain-link fence. We rolled on the floor. I managed to snag a luggage bar and hold on. Paulie, Choke, and the bus driver Steve grabbed on to the seats.

"Hold on!" Gunner shouted.

Man please. "Way ahead of you, baby!" I shouted back.

Gunner ripped the bus out of the battered fence, tearing off part of the bumper. He roared toward the entry gate and rammed through the "down" arm, which splintered and crackled on impact. Gunner drove toward the auto pound where cars are towed after they're ticketed for illegal parking at the terminal.

There were a bunch of cars, city tow trucks, and police vehicles. Gunner stopped about half a block away.

"Why are you stopping?" Steve found the courage to get up off the floor and sit on the hard, plastic seats.

Gunner turned around. "I doubt they'll be shooting at us so close to the cops. They can't be that crazy, can they?"

Steve grimaced in disgust and then started to leave.

Paulie grabbed his arm and yanked Steve down next to him, putting an elbow against his chest. "Did you forget about our little conversation?"

"You can't keep me here. Somebody's ticked AT YOU and I don't wanna be nowhere around."

I wasn't in the mood to hear his whining and neither was Choke. *"Cállate!"* he told him.

The bus driver did shut up. Then I began laying down the law.

"Listen. We came to talk to you about Mandy and Herc—"

"I TOLD YOU TO LEAVE ME OUT OF IT."

"Cállate pronto!"

Again he did as Choke ordered.

I told Steve, "Look. If I wanna play games, I go play Chutes and Ladders with my nephew. We've got a friend who could get killed. Not to mention a bunch of other innocent folks too. Now we've GOT TO FIND Mandy. We know she's with Herc. When we went looking for them at her place, we found a dead man in the bedroom."

The bus driver started panting.

"Then we come here and we're told you're tight with the couple. We're on the right track because now somebody's trying to scare us off, but we don't scare. What kind of trouble are Mandy and Herc into?"

Steve put his head in his hands. Sweat was pouring down his face. He wiped it away and said, "Okay."

"Okay what?" Gunner asked. "Mandy and Herc are dealing?"

Steve nodded.

"How?" I shrugged.

"She was a flight attendant," he said like *duh.*

Then I thought about what Mandy's co-worker said, *and she makes a lot of flights to Mexico.* "She was smuggling in drugs? From Mexico?"

"Yeah. And Herc was moving them. Didn't say how or where. He let it slip one night while we were having a few brews. It was a while back though."

"What else?" I prodded.

"Nothing else. Not really. A couple of days ago I hit his cell and he told me that he and Mandy had to lay low. She got fired and their drug thing was all screwed up and some people were pissed off."

"What's the cell number?"

Steve told me. "But it's no good. I've been trying. It's disconnected."

"Do you know where they might be hiding?"

"No. Haven't seen or talked to them since; didn't get an answer at Mandy's place either. I'm not playing around here. I REALLY don't know where they are! You gotta believe me. Look." He pulled out a wallet with some photos. "I got a wife and kids. I don't need any trouble."

The photo of the kids was cute as pie. Steve was dressed in a clown suit next to them. A birthday cake was in the background. "I'm just trying to take care of my family. I've told you all I know, swear to God."

Paulie calmed him. "Okay, kid. Relax. We believe you."

"But what about the people looking for Mandy and Herc? What about them? You came to me. Will they? I got kids. I can't go home and chance that some thug is gonna come around asking questions about stuff *I don't know jack about.*"

I advised him, "Calm down, Steve. Let me make a couple of calls. I have some cop friends who'll pick you up inside the auto pound over there. They'll take you to a motel where the cops stash a lot of witnesses and stuff. Nothing fancy but you don't look like the *Donald Trump type* so you should be fine. Just stay there overnight. By that time, we should have found Mandy and cleared up this mess."

Steve sighed in relief. "Thanks." Then as an afterthought: "Suppose YOU DON'T find Mandy and Herc? *What then?*"

"Then," I told him, "one of our best friends and a bank full of hostages will be killed."

"So you see," Choke said, "WE'VE GOT TO FIND HER."

Gunner's cell phone rang. He answered it. Then he handed the phone to me. "Who is it, Gunner?"

"The morgue. Who else?"

The morgue sounded like Motown.

We hightailed it there. We were in the area where my man Ju Wung worked. An assistant brought us in. Wung was on the way. He had the radio going, playing a dusties station that was doing an hour-long set of '60s dance music.

Choke, the Dick Clark of TV news, started to do a little dance.

I teased him, "Whatdaya call that?"

"Aww chica, you don't know nothing about this. This is before your time. This dance is called 'Kill that Roach.'"

Choke's hips were swaying and he was stomping his feet.

I told him, "I guess Raid sales were down in the barrio that year, huh Choke?"

"In the ghetto too, chica. In the ghetto too."

Ju Wung came in. I like his taste in music IN ADDI-TION to the fact that he's just a *bad boy*. Badder than all those guys you see on cable news theorizing about the Laci Peterson case and the Kobe Bryant case and all that. He was a forensic scientist from the part on the top of his head down to the tips of his toenails. I'd ask him all the time about letting me hook him up with the networks so he could get famous like some of those other folks. Wung wasn't feeling me on that. And ya know I was halfway happy because he was a fabulous source and a heck of a friend.

"Hi Wung. Remember these guys?" I pointed out the Video Cowboys. Reintroduced everyone. "They're helping me out. I'm trying to find Mandy."

Wung pointed out a little black-and-white TV, no more than ten inches, sitting on a counter. "I know. I saw your special report."

"You watch me on that? I probably look like one of the singing raisins on that little old thing."

He laughed.

"You, my friend, look good on any size TV and even better in person. I know I'm a little old for you but I've got to ask. When will you marry me?"

"You tell me what I need to know to help Zeke and I'll marry you and be barefoot and pregnant in the kitchen." I paused. Then WE ALL looked at each other and said together, "NOT!"

Then Wung got down to business.

He walked us over to a table with a body on it. A shirt was hung on a hanger hooked onto the countertop. Wung picked up a spritz can, like he was about to water a flower. "The victim's shirt. Splattered with blood, of course. But add a little spray of this—"

"Which," I joked, "IS NOT stain-remover Tide."

"No, it's cobalt thiocyanate." Wung sprayed it. "It highlights the presence of a very illegal powdery substance."

"Cocaine," Paulie guessed.

"Right," Wung said. "It was just a little on the shirt. Like maybe he picked it up through minor contact with something. Or someone. There was no sign of drug use on the body. Speaking of bodies, anyone here squeamish?"

Not a mumbling word was uttered. Wung pulled back the sheet. I have to admit, the boy looked better after an autopsy than he did on the floor of Mandy's apartment. That's real.

Paulie even commented, "You cleaned him up pretty good."

Wung answered solemnly. "I respect the dead. They've provided me with quite a nice living over the years. Now Georgia. First, let's talk about the cause of death."

"I just assumed he died from a gunshot wound." I asked the Video Cowboys, "Didn't we see a bullet hole?"

They said yes. Wung confirmed that we weren't crazy and seeing things, before he explained further.

"You saw a bullet hole in the side. Here," he pointed with a metal probe. "Not lethal, Georgia. It's what's called a 'pain wound' in organized circles."

"Organized circles?"

"The mob," Paulie said.

Choke teased, "Your peoples, Paulie."

"Stop breaking my balls, Choke. Go 'head, Wung."

"That's not the only pain wound on the body. There's more. A lot more, Georgia."

"Then somebody should have heard something, Wung, yelling or screaming. Shouldn't they?"

"No, because this wound was first." Wung pointed to the murder victim's throat. "It's partially crushed. See the narrow indentation?"

"Yeah," I said. "His voice box is squashed. What did they hit him with?"

"Guess."

Like I had a clue? I looked at the Video Cowboys for help.

Paulie guessed. "A bat handle?"

Wung shook his head no.

Gunner guessed next. "A hunk of pipe?"

Wung shook his head.

Choke's turn. "Something in the apartment, like a curtain rod or something?"

Wung liked to tease. "So much for polling the audience, Georgia. Wanna try a lifeline?"

"I give."

"Who pumps iron?" Wung asked the Video Cowboys. Gunner leaned over the body and examined it carefully. "A circular weight?"

"Right! Five pounds to be exact."

"So," I asked, "what was the cause of death?"

"Down here on the rib cage, these puncture marks. One of them hit a lung. Notice the size and the indentation. It's a common tool. You can find it in the house or in the garage. Got a guess, Georgia?"

I looked closely.

It was narrow and had a series of grooves. "A Phillips screwdriver?"

"Good job!" Wung said. "You win a prize. But that comes later. The wound in the lung area is deep, eight inches in."

"Okay," I said. "The average person can't take that kind of interruption of the nervous system without going into shock."

"Or more simply," Wung said, "cardiac arrest."

Paulie shrugged. "So they tortured the poor mope til his heart gave out."

Wung nodded.

I asked him, "So what's my prize?"

"Our counterparts in the P.D. are running his fingerprints for ID purposes. I've got a friend over there who's waiting on you, Georgia. He'll help."

"I can't go to the police crime lab, Wung. I've got a little problem."

"Like what?"

"Like the cops are looking for me . . . There's a warrant out for my arrest."

"You've got to be kidding, Georgia."

"No, *esse*," Choke said. "She's for real."

Wung was puzzled. "What for?"

"I had a run-in with the top cop running this hostage operation. Name's Bill Whelk."

Wung threw out his nickname. "Wild Bill? Say no more. Let me call my guy." Wung made the call, talked to his friend, then hung up. "Says he's working on it and will fax over what he finds. Hang tight. He's close."

Gunner asked, "How's that fingerprint jive work anyway, Wung?"

"There are forty-four million prints in the FBI database."

Paulie joked, "That's about half the number of prints that were on my car windows last week when I carpooled my grandkids to the circus."

Wung went on. "That's a lot of people to weed through. So you look for matches in curves and ridges. In Europe, they have a strict points system. Some places there use twelve or more points of similarity before a print is labeled a match. Here in America it's not that intense. A computer spits out the prints that SEEM CLOSE. Afterward an examiner checks them by hand."

Choke frowned at Wung. "Sounds like a pain in the butt. And what kind of time are we talking about?"

"Days. Hours. Minutes. My guy is the fastest and the most accurate tech in the department. *When he knows, you'll know.*"

"My man!" I gave him a hug and a kiss on the cheek.

"Aww," Paulie teased. "Ain't that sweet."

Wung playfully teased Paulie back, faking like he expected a show of affection from him. "What?" he said to Paulie. "No love?"

Paulie held up his hand, "Hey. Georgia throws kisses. I throw beatings."

Suddenly the fax machine started gurgling. We all hovered around while it labored and moaned, giving birth to a brand-new clue.

I read it.

Choke said it. "There's a definite match."

Paulie cheered it. "Yeah baby!"

Gunner questioned it. "What's a parole officer doing mixed up with Mandy and Herc?"

Paulie shrugged, "You want my two cents? Maybe he was a drug dealer too."

So now we went about trying to *turn two cents into a buck.*

Because the victim worked in law enforcement it was easy to get all his vital stats. His name was Xavier Kurt. He was thirty-five years old and lived on the near north side. Worked for ten years for the county parole office. Left behind a wife and two kids.

I asked the Video Cowboys, "Who's got some props at the parole office?"

Gunner fit the bill this time. He had a nephew and a cousin who worked parole. We were able to catch his nephew, who worked out of another office BUT who *had juice* because he was a supervisor, PLUS his father-in-law used to run the entire department before he retired.

"Uncle Gun. Why don't you come around sometime?" Gunner's nephew was named Jeff. He's got thick, wavy Bermuda brown hair. I put Jeff around fortyish. He's a little on the short side, but throws off serious stature. Bulky chest and arms make his shirt fit tight; that puts his bulging abs and impressive physique straight *on front street*. Jeff wore loose tapered slacks and a pair of socks with Daffy Duck on them. He noticed me checking out his Looney Tunes legwear.

Jeff hiked up his pant's leg. "My daughter gave 'em to me. Kid wakes you up and asks you to wear their present, whatcha gonna say?"

I liked him.

"Uncle Gunner, she's a doll. You oughta see her. But she's growing up without you. Don't be so distant. You and Dad are brothers. I know you guys don't get along but please—"

"Hey Jeff. We need that info. Later for the personal stuff, okay?"

Jeff's chest rolled as a heavy sigh hung in the air. Gunner cupped the back of Jeff's neck. "Still working out like I showed you years ago, huh kid?"

His nephew smiled, then turned toward a hallway. "Come on."

He took us into his office and closed the door. The radio was on. "I've been listening to the news. Haven't heard anything new on the hostage situation."

"No news is good news," I sighed. "We told Brett to be patient and hold tight."

Choke nodded. "And you know Zeke. *That loco hombre?* C'mon. He's in there talking the guy's head off, probably got him laughing by now trying to keep everything cool."

"Well," Jeff said, "everything's been cool around here. Nothing's broke about this Xavier Kurt. When a parole officer gets hurt, it's devastating—now one of our own is dead. *Whew.* It's gonna be nuts around here when everybody hears. But tell me, how'd you guys find out so fast?"

"Stumbled onto the body," I said wryly. "It was a bad trip, Jeff. Excuse the pun. What were you able to find out about Kurt?"

"I have some friends who work with the guy. I asked about a couple of other people too, ya know, trying to make it look good. They said he was upright. Did his job. Backed up the other P.O.'s. So I doubt if he was dirty."

Gunner balked. "Coulda been filthy and they didn't know it. It's not like the guy is gonna take out an ad in the *Sun-Times* saying he's drug dealing. Know what I'm saying, Jeff?"

"Yeah, but ah, sometimes you can smell dirt though. Around here? Yeah you can. *You can.* Parole officers lean on each other more than cops do as a whole. Cops usually lean on their partner. Parole officers lean on every SINGLE body in the office. It ain't a pretty job, Uncle Gunner."

"What do ya mean?"

"You're NOT QUITE a cop but you still LOOK LIKE a cop, carrying a gun, able to violate a parolee and send them back to jail. Most of the ex-cons hate you, fear you, and the knuckleheads on the street think you're weak; just a pencil-pushing police plaything and they wanna challenge you left and right."

I felt for him. "I know it's gotta be tough, Jeff. Dealing with so many people too. And getting into their personal lives, as seamy as they are most of the time."

He nodded. "But that's the territory. One of the friends I asked about Kurt said that he was working on some kind of big case. That one of his parolees was mixed up in something bad; that kinda had the guy walking around on eggshells."

Gunner asked his nephew, "Did they say what?"

"Didn't say WHAT, Uncle Gun, or WHO for that matter, BUT I can narrow it down some for you."

"How?" Gunner asked.

Jeff sat down at his desk and hit a button on the computer. He slid a stack of files off to the side. "Step around the madness."

The Video Cowboys and I did just that. We huddled around him like he was the star quarterback and we were the offensive line. "Our new computer system cost an arm and a leg and we didn't get our raises, so everybody around here hates it."

"Not my nephew though," Gunner said to us. "Know anybody who likes being called a computer geek?"

Jeff laughed.

Paulie growled. "I hate computers. And anything where the people who love it are called 'junkies,' 'geeks,' and 'hackers' has gotta be a bunch of CRAP."

Jeff grinned, shook his head, and continued. "Now, because I'm a supervisor, I have access to the files of the other P.O.'s via computer. Not the entire file. I'd have to get that from the P.O. themselves. But I can see which cascs each P.O. has been assigned and which ones they've called up the most."

Interesting, I thought. Computers were becoming the time clocks of the twenty-first century. "So what's the setup?"

"They have to call up the file to log in how much

time they spend on each parolee. That's where the red alert system kicks in. That means that if I call up a P.O.'s caseload, the computer will highlight in red the cases that he or she is spending the most time on."

"And that's important because?" I asked.

"Helps to track the REAL troublemakers. As a supervisor you can review a summary file on the case and kinda ask the P.O. if they need help or share some ideas. Some people DON'T KNOW when to ask for help and others are TOO PROUD to ask."

"So," Paulie said. "Type in the dead P.O.'s name and see what pops. This case that had him running scared might have a connection to Mandy and Herc."

Jeff typed in Xavier Kurt. The names of his parolees came up and *every last one of them was* RED.

Paulie huffed, "What did I say, I hate computers!"

"It's a glitch," Jeff's voice warbled with worry, then pride. *"A glitch. But I'll fix it."*

The rat-a-tat-tat of breaking news suddenly erupted on the radio. The anchor's baritone voice kicked in. "We interrupt this broadcast to bring you this special update on the hostage situation at Lake Michigan Bank."

The room fainted into silence. We stared at the little radio as the broadcaster's words eked out.

The standoff has been going on now for more than five hours. Just minutes ago the gunman inside the bank tossed out a videotape. There was a note attached saying that on the tape was an urgent message for Channel 8 reporter Georgia Barnett. The police WILL NOT say what is on the tape NOR will they release it to the media to air. They're holding it until Ms. Barnett turns herself in. Apparently there is a warrant out for her arrest.

That's a heck of a choice, huh?

Find out what's on the tape and go to jail OR keep taking shots at finding Mandy and take a chance that there's nothing important on that tape.

Choke rattled off something low and sinister-sounding in Spanish. I looked at him: "I don't even WANNA KNOW what you said."

Paulie huffed. "You gotta choose, Georgia."

"I can't."

The Video Cowboys looked at one another. Gunner took the lead. "You want us to choose for you?"

Did I? Could I be that passive in such an important life-or-death situation? Was I that unsure of my own judgment? Was I that afraid of making a mistake that I might not be able to live with?

No. I couldn't go out like that, not taking charge of my own destiny.

Weren't things already out of control?

I had already had a gun pointed at me and been threatened with death inside that bank, a hostage just trying to survive. I get sprung but at what cost? To be sent on what mission?

A search and survive mission. Had to search for the gunman's daughter Mandy in order for one of my best friends to survive. Zeke was still stuck with being a hostage; the man's got a gun pointed at him and a bomb set to go off to kill him and anybody else inside that bank.

I'm on my mission, trying to do my thing and save the day and who is supposed to help me? The police, of course. But who ends up hating on a sister and blocking my flow? Wild Bill Whelk.

He's one of the city's top cops and I had pissed him off SO MUCH that he wanted to have me locked up.

I thought about it a second and my choice was clear. We'd run out of hot clues. We're onto something with Xavier Kurt, but what? I needed to find out what was on that tape.

"I'm going in."

Choke moaned, *"Aye-aye! Muy loco."*

"It's not as crazy as it sounds. That tape Brett sent out has got to be important. The note said 'urgent,' right? I turn myself in and Wild Bill gets his jollies by sending a message to the media. He's trying to embarrass me before making me get Brett in a position where he can have a sniper take him out. Well I don't care what he says, I ain't doing that."

The Video Cowboys knew me by now. Paulie sneered, "Just like the wife, can't tell her nothing." Then he winked. "We'll keep working angles here."

"When we find out what's on that tape, I'll figure out how to hook back up with you guys. Keep Clarice in the loop. She'll be our connection with each other until we can get back together. See ya soon."

"Bill said we'd get you sooner or later."

Captain Daniel Carey was doing the talking. Doug advised me earlier that he was Wild Bill Whelk's right-hand man on the force. Carey was throwing off MUCH ATTITUDE. *And why not?* He had the upper hand. We were at police headquarters in District A, just half a mile away from the bank and the hostage situation. I had turned myself in and the cops had me sitting in an interrogation room.

Captain Carey was an average guy in build and features. He was an old-school Irish cop. He wore a uniform. Starched.

Carey played with his thick mustache and growled, "You look awful stupid sitting here. And why? 'Cause you're hardheaded, that's why. This is no place for you."

Captain Carey wasn't lying. The interrogation room smelled like one of my man Doug's sweatshirts after a workout. That's Funk with a capital K. The walls were so dirty I wasn't sure if the original color was blue or gray. On the right side of the room, there were a couple of holes in the wall. One was perfectly round like somebody's head; *hat size extra large y'all.* The other was a footprint: spike-heel pumps, *size off the rack.*

I was sitting facing a glass, which you know was a two-way dealio so NO TELLING who was sitting back there *getting their jollies off* seeing a diva TV reporter slumming behind bars.

Windows? If that's what you wanna call them. There were two. They were about as clear as ice blocks and shoved all crooked into the wall with bars covering them. The floor was linoleum, swarthy as mud, tattered on the corners or missing altogether in some spots. So I just glared at Captain Carey, halfway hot because I didn't cotton to being called stupid.

"Whataya gaping at?" he asked.

"Believe it or not, you're the best-looking thing in the room—*which ain't saying much.*"

"You gotta smart mouth, Ms. Barnett, but can you back it up?"

"You didn't catch me. I turned myself in, remember?"

"Doesn't matter HOW you got reeled in lady, Chicago P.D. baited the hook."

"Let's skip the games. How are the hostages?"

Captain Carey pulled up a chair and propped his leg up in it. "They're all still okay. We tossed a note tied to a weight up against the door. He had the pregnant woman stick her head out, grab it, and take it inside."

"What did the note say?"

"We told him that we would trade him a hostage for food. Send out a hostage, tell us what he wants to eat, and we'll send it in."

"Well whose idea was that?"

"Bill's."

I rolled my eyes. "So what happened?"

"Nothing yet. He's still waiting to see that tape he sent out aired on TV."

"The one for me? Marked urgent?"

"That's the one."

"But that's our deal, captain. You gotta play it. We're communicating with each other back and forth via those tapes. What's on it?"

"Gibberish."

"Show it to me."

"When skis go on sale in hell." Captain Carey growled, "Do I look like I pee sitting down?"

"No," I snapped. "Laying down maybe. Did you wet the bed?"

"Smart mouth. Keep talking. If you had played ball and followed Bill's plan those hostages wouldn't still be stuck in there with a gun on 'em and a bomb that could go off and blow everybody straight to hell."

I caught something. "Bill's plan, you said, as in NOT OUR PLAN. Do you REALLY agree with how he's handling this, huh?"

"We have a job to do, Ms. Barnett. I take orders. And we do whatever it takes to get the job done."

I cracked, "You sound like Jack Nicholson in *A Few Good Men*. Next you're gonna tell me that *I want you on that wall, that I need you on that wall.*"

"Jack Nicholson, huh? We'll let's talk about that place deep down inside he says SOFTIES like you don't wanna talk about at parties."

"You don't know me, captain."

"I know we're in this waiting game 'CAUSE of you. Too chicken to try and bait this guy to the door or a window. You coulda saved us a lot of time and him the anguish of digging in."

"You want me to be the bait that gets somebody killed?"

"Not just anybody. A gunman. A hostage taker. A bank robber."

Captain Carey was breaking me down with this guilt thing. *Can't let him break me down, I thought.* He continued to try to work me.

"What about this, Georgia? You make the call and I promise that I'll talk Bill into ordering the snipers to go for a disabling shot and not a direct kill. How's that?"

"I don't know, captain. All this is just too crazy for me."

"Listen, it's still daylight and that's the only way to get a clear shot; after that all bets are off."

"What do you mean all bets are off?"

"Nothing." He took his leg out of the chair then slammed the chair up against the table. "I'm tired of talking."

"But I'm not tired of listening. Talk to me, captain. Aren't you looking for his daughter?"

"You bet we are! But we can't just stand around like wallflowers at a school dance 'til we find her! Suppose she's out of state? Suppose she's seen what's going on and is too scared to come forward? You've been snooping around. You know about Brett, you've been out to the hospital; you've seen his record. And whoever those guys were with you—all of you are damn lucky that the hospital was too scared of bad publicity to press trespassing and assault charges."

I did some quick thinking. This was going nowhere. But Doug said Carey was on the up and up. He also said *to play* to him. And what better way to p*lay* to him than to use a comparison I knew he'd understand.

"I did what I had to do to help my partner. Wouldn't you bend a few rules to do what you could to save your partner? Huh, Captain?"

He straightened up. "Your partner?"

"Zeke Rouster. The hostage that's a cameraman?"

"What about him?"

"In TV, a reporter and cameraman are partners. Just like a police unit."

Captain Carey's eyes softened. *I'd hit a nerve.*

"You had to have a partner when you rode the streets in a squad. Who had your back?"

He pulled out a package of cigarettes. Lit one. "Arnie."

"Zeke is my Arnie. What's Arnie doing now?"

Captain Carey took a drag off the cigarette. "Lost him a couple of years ago. He and a rookie got killed while out training. They got caught up in a robbery."

"I remember that! It happened at a west side grocery store. Your guy took the shooter out before he died on the way to the hospital. I covered that story."

Our eyes met.

Suddenly the door of the interrogation room opened. "Hey boss," a detective shouted. "You gotta see this. Some-

thing's shaking at the bank. Her station's got it on now.
They got one of those chopper cameras up in the air."

Captain Carey bolted for the door. I came behind
him. He looked over his shoulder. The detective blocked
the door. Captain Carey growled, "Aww, let her come."

I followed them to a corner of the detective squad
where everyone was hovered around a thirteen-inch TV
sitting on top of a microwave.

The television was on. I recognized video from our
chopper cam with the logo in the corner. The video
showed the top floor of the building. There was a little
hutch-like structure with a door in the center of the roof.
Then the chopper swung back and you could see the
front door on the street level. Pete was still anchoring
our coverage. He began describing for the audience what
they were seeing.

This is a bird's eye view of Lake Michigan Bank
where a hostage standoff has been going on since this
morning. Just moments ago, a shot was heard.

Oh my God, I thought. *What set Brett off? Who did he
shoot? Did Zeke try to take the gun away and get shot?* I
held my breath.

Look in the corner of your screen. You see police officers advancing slowly. Right at this moment is when
the front door opens and a man stumbles out. Then suddenly collapses.

The door of the bank opened. A man did stumble out.
You could see blood as the chopper camera zoomed in. I

squinted. "That looks like the bike messenger. The one who pulled the gun and tried to shoot Brett."

Channel 8 News has learned that the man is a hostage. He is being rushed to the hospital suffering from a minor gunshot wound. No word yet on his condition. All we know right now is that he works for a bike messenger service. His name is being withheld by police.

One of the detectives noticed something on the video. He pointed to it with his thumb, like a hitchhiker. "Look at that. There's something on his shirt. What is it?"
I couldn't tell what it was.

There was a note pinned to the hostage's clothes. Channel 8 News has learned exclusively what was on that note. It said: PLAY THE TAPE. We believe that message refers to a tape that was sent out earlier and marked URGENT for our own Georgia Barnett. Chicago police refused to release the tape to us to air UNTIL Barnett turned herself in to face obstruction of justice charges. A charge they leveled while she was doing her job—covering the story PLUS trying to help free the hostages—one of them a Channel 8 cameraman. Barnett turned herself in just a short time ago. No word yet on whether or not police will turn over the tape as promised. Stay tuned. We're staying with the story and will bring you ALL the latest as soon as it happens. Now back to our regularly scheduled program.

"The case is cooking now," one of the detectives said.
"You know what that means," another added.

"Yeah," Captain Carey said matter-of-factly. "Bill is blowing a gasket. I'm gonna head over to the command center and see what he plans to do next."

What I planned on doing next was *make Captain Carey my messenger boy.* So I said, "And while you're there, tell Bill I kept my end of the bargain. I turned myself in. So he should release the tape so the media can air it."

Like my grandmama used to say, *Shut my mouth. I drew everybody's attention to fine little old me.*

"WHAT ABOUT HER, CAP?" one of the detectives asked. "What about the charges?"

"We can't drop 'em. AT LEAST not yet. It'll look like we're scared of the media. Do this. Push her through the system speedo style, half an hour or less. Make it comfortable, no funny stuff like putting her in with the pickpockets and the pros. Somebody get with the state's attorney too—make sure there's no bond issue. I'm sure Ms. Barnett has someone who can bail her out ASAP."

15

"*Georgia-Georgia!* And Mama always said I was the bad twin."

My sister Peaches was obnoxious. She stood in front of me grinning from ear to ear, hands on her bodacious hips, big hair, mucho Fashion Fair makeup on her face. Everybody joked that, for twins, we looked about as much alike as a penny and a dime. Peaches had her tongue pressed up against the gap between her two front teeth snorting giggles at me.

"'Member that boyfriend I had in high school that got arrested? You and Mama talked about me like a dog for bailing him out. How's bailing you out any different?"

"I went to jail on principle."

"Him too—for jumping on the principal."

"You know what . . ." I let the phrase simmer out of my mouth. "*You are working my nerves.*"

"Georgia the ingrate. You oughta be on your knees

THANKFUL that it's me bailing you out and not Mama."

She had a point. We began walking out.

"Mama always told ME not to call her number or her name if I got locked up while hanging out with the bad boys. You being *Glenda the Good Twin*, you probably never got that speech, huh?"

"You know what you're gonna get, Peaches? You're gonna get my foot straight up your—"

"Mama!" Zack came running over to us. Peaches had left her son with one of the female detectives. She picked him up. He was sucking his thumb, eyes twinkling. "Look who Mommie has with her!" she told him.

Zack stopped sucking his thumb and said, "Auntie Jailbird!"

Peaches nearly choked . . . *choked on laughter*.

My eyes bucked and I know I was looking all crazy at the child.

"What did you say little bad boy?"

"Auntie Jail—"

Peaches clapped her hand over his mouth. "You're playing with fire, son. Cool it."

Then I started tapping my foot. "Where'd he get THAT from?"

"Eyeeee, don't know. Kids repeat stuff. You know how it is, twin. But not to change the subject . . ."

"But you're gonna change the subject. What, Peaches?"

"You look a hot mess! Stress is all over your face."

"Like I needed to hear that."

"Sorry sister-twin. I'm praying for Zeke."

"I know. Me too."

"Save some prayers for yo'self, child. 'Cause when

Mama hears about you going to jail she's gonna throw a natural fit, you hear me?"

"And you're going to be there laughing your butt off!"

"Aww yeah, G. It'll be good to see YOU get in trouble for a change. Speaking of change. When you gonna gimme my bail money back?"

I did the tilt-a-whirl black girl head swirl. "Peaches. I KNOW you are not asking me that! AS MUCH money as you have borrowed from me and not paid back? Let's see . . . There's the money for your back rent. Then there's the money to fix up the club two years ago . . . And more recently . . ."

"I ain't talking about THAT MONEY past, Georgia. I'm talking about THIS MONEY present."

"Quit it, Peaches. Just get me to the station. I've gotta check in with Clarice, eyeball this new tape, and catch up with the Video Cowboys."

When we got to the parking lot, Peaches stopped at a Mercedes SUV, black on black.

It was so pretty and so out of Peaches' league that I forgot the basic rules of grammar. I said, "NO YOU AIN'T!"

"YES I'M IS," Peaches said, doing the same thing. She laughed. "No, not really. I just borrowed it from a guy I'm dating. Get in."

I did. "What kind of a man would let you drive a car like this?"

"One that's whupped."

"I never dated a man who let me borrow a car like this."

"That's why I'm the 'peach' and you're the 'state,'

Georgia. I'm round and sweet. You're dry and flat."

I can't believe this crazy woman. I just laughed at her highfalutin nonsense. "Drive, drama queen. Drive."

Once I got dropped off at Channel 8, I made my way inside to the newsroom. My people down south love to say, *Sometimes you get the bear and sometimes the bear gets you.*

In my case, the bear was Brett in the bank but here at Channel 8, the bear is Halo Bingington, my boss. Not that Bing is a bad man, mind you. He's just too intense, without a lick of common sense. For example, common sense would tell you not to mess with me with all that I'm going through and STILL have to get through on this story. So if I were YOU, and saw ME coming, I'd *back up Jack or hit the road Joe.* Instead *Bing tried to start a thing.*

"Georgia!" he shouted.

The man was coming out of the bathroom, shaking his wet hands, and then wiping them on the sides of his slacks. Bing is Fred Flintstone. I don't know y'all . . . something about socks seem to bother the man. His ashy ankles are always showing beneath his heavily cuffed khaki pants. Bing's blue blazer and white shirt often re-mind me of the senior class president at a prep school; a president everyone picked BECAUSE he'd get everything done—which, somehow, outweighed the fact that he got on your last nerve by oh, about *half a smidgen.*

"Georgia—good to see you."

Cool, right? Stop there.

"Follow me. I want to tell you how I want this story covered the rest of the way. You're doing fine BUT—"

Aww see. He's a DEAD MAN WALKING and don't even know it. Not today Mr. Nit-Pick. "Bing. I'm hustling and pulling every string that I can. I don't have the time OR the spirit to be lectured right now. I have one of the highest popularity ratings in the city and an Emmy too. Just this once . . . and EVEN THOUGH you are the boss . . . PLEASE back OFF."

Bing was so surprised that I told him to back off me that he forgot how to work his feet, LITERALLY. He stopped cold, then when he tried to take a step, *Bing tripped over his feet and fell flat on his face.*

I held my laughter until I went through the door that led to the newsroom, and then I burst out with a mixture of laughter and tears. I was cracking from the stress. The newsroom was buzzing like a beehive. Most of the reporters were out. There were writers at their desks, banging out copy. Researchers were running around passing out press releases and court documents. Cameramen burst through side doors, tossing tapes to managers. Editors sat in their glassed-in rooms, whirling tape back and forth, searching for the best shot to help tell the story.

My desk was piled high with old scripts and tapes. I love funky picture frames. I had one shaped like Mickey Mouse with pictures of me, my nephew Zack, Mama, and Peaches in it. I had a heart-shaped one with Doug and I hugged-up at the beach. I made a little ledge on top of my cubicle with the help of *Design on a Dime* and $19.99 at Home Depot. On that ledge I put what are called mike flags. Those are the little squares that you see on a reporter's handheld mike when he or she is going live. It usually has the station's call letters or network logo on it. I collected one from each of the stations I had worked in—including

my college television station. The little colored squares
with different numbers—2, 11, or letters like WMB or
WPK—resembled some kind of a Rubik's Cube resume
of where my career has taken me.

The blinking red light on my desk phone caught my
eye. I checked my voice mail quickly, deleting the message as soon as I determined that the caller would not
impact my life this instant or save Zeke's either for that
matter. I finally played one that made me smile.

"Baby, it's me. Doug. Hit me up and let me know
what's going on. I'm worried."

*Ain't it a blessing to have a fine brother worrying
about a sister?*

I dialed Doug's cell.

"What's going on, girl? Are you okay?"

"Yeah, Doug. "

"I mean what the hell is up? One of my boys sent a
text message. He said *you were in jail.*"

"I was. I made Wild Bill mad and he put a warrant
out for my arrest."

"For what?!"

"Allegedly obstructing justice."

"That's it. I'm coming home."

Oh Lord. "Cool it, Shaft. We both know you couldn't
possibly get here in time to help anyway. Plus, you'd
jeopardize your job."

"Yeah, but it would be worth it just to kick Whelk's
tail."

"I feel you baby and I love you for it. I'm fine. I'm
on the case just trying my best to get Zeke outta there.
Just keep praying for us."

"I will. But be careful. I like my man Zeke and all, so don't get me wrong BUT I don't want NOTHING tragic to happen to you, baby."

Even in a life-and-death situation like this, a self-respecting sister had to pitch one underhanded. I cooed, "You sound like a man who might wanna jump the broom?"

"Huh? Whatcha say baby, my cell is conking out. Can't understand a thing you're saying. Be safe! Bye."

MEN. Scared to go to the preacher.

I hung up. That's when I spotted Clarice. I nearly snatched her out of her 'fro when I came up behind her. "Where's the tape?"

Clarice clasped her hands to her chest and sighed, "You scared the living stew out of me. Who taught you how to walk up on somebody, the grim reaper?"

My adrenaline was rushing. *"Sorry, sorry, sorry . . . Where's the tape?"*

"On it's way. Be here any second. Here."

Clarice handed me a new cell phone since mine was still stuck at the bank. "Did you see Bing? He was waiting for you."

I grinned, reimagining him falling on his face. "I saw him."

Clarice followed up. "Then you know. After you do a piece on set for the update, he wants a live pop from you for the afternoon break. He wants something new. Anything."

"Gotcha. Heard from the Video Cowboys?"

"Yeah, they're on the way in too. Didn't have much luck at the parole office. Apparently the system—"

"Had red-flagged all of the dead officer's parolees! The system is down."

"Right, Georgia. They did say that they were able to pull together a list of his recent parolees. You know, names and addresses; kinda like a profile sheet for each person. Just in case one of them has some kind of a connection to Herc and Mandy."

"Cool. The Video Cowboys brought you up to speed."

"I'm on the case, girl. I know where EVERY last body is buried in this newsroom, who did the killing, who performed the autopsy, who dug the hole, and who sprung for the headstone. I'm not here to play!"

"Me neither, Clarice."

An intern came running in with a tape. "Fresh from the cops," he shouted.

"Throw!" I said.

He tossed the tape to me underhanded. I caught it. "Let's roll this bad boy and see what's on it that's so urgent."

"What could it be, Georgia?"

"Clarice, I'm here to tell ya. *I'm a black girl who loves fine housewares but I have yet to find and purchase a crystal ball. We won't know a thang 'til we look.*"

"Not without our eyeballs!" It was Paulie leading the charge of the Video Cowboys.

I hugged my guys.

"How was the slammer?" Gunner joked.

"Sorry: saving it for my memoirs." I waved for everyone to follow me. We headed for a bay, which is a small room with equipment that can record audio and cut videotape.

"May I?" Gunner took the videotape out of my hand and plugged it into the machine. He hit the play button and quickly adjusted the volume, which started out as tone—then the color, which was a set of bars. Then it faded to black. "Here it comes," Gunner said. "Ready?" *We weren't ready. Not for what we saw.*

AFTER WE WATCHED IT TWICE, Gunner looked up at Clarice and me and said, "Can you air that?"

Clarice snorted, "You ain't hip to reality TV?"

I answered for Gunner. "The Video Cowboys are old-school. But it's a new day, gentlemen; it airs uncut but I'm coming right behind it with my story. My story will update Brett on where we are on finding Mandy."

Twenty minutes later we hit the air at the end of the four o'clock news. I was sitting on set but the director opened with our special report slate, which then dissolved to a single shot of Pete.

Good afternoon everyone. I'm Peter Bradford.

We interrupt our regularly scheduled broadcast to bring you the latest on the hostage situation at Lake Michigan Bank. Just a short time ago, we received a videotape that was made by the man holding hostages at bay with a gun and a bomb. Chicago police were withholding that tape until Channel 8's Georgia Barnett turned herself in to face obstruction of justice charges. She joins us now to show us what was on that urgent videotape AND to update us on the search for the gunman's daughter. Georgia?

The director took a two shot of me and Pete.

Thank you Pete.

I turned from the two shot to a side camera that would put me on a solo angle, one on one, with the audience.

As those of you following our coverage already know, I was a hostage inside Lake Michigan Bank too. The gunman, now identified as Brett Andronte, released me in the hopes that I, along with police, could find his daughter Mandy. If she is found, he has promised to release the hostages UNHARMED before turning himself in. The police issued a warrant for my arrest for allegedly obstructing justice. Charges are pending but the police turned over the tape marked urgent. And urgent it is:

Roll the videotape. It was Brett going on a tirade inside the bank, angry and frustrated about his life. He was ranting and kicking over chairs, breaking vases, and tossing picture frames up against the walls:

What the hell is happening out there?! We've been in here for hours and my daughter still isn't here! I'm struggling. God I'm struggling. I can't seem to win. No matter what I do or say or try or who I help. Everything is going round and round in my head and my heart is racing. I've got this gun and this bomb and I don't know what to do. What to do?

Zeke pans from Brett to the rear of the bank to the room where the hostages are being held. They stand against the glass, hands pressed up against the transparent, taunt, tone-barrier surface, silent yet their bodies

scream with fearful posture. Brett in his tirade moves to
the back of the bank; he stands and points the gun. Like
figures in an encapsulated toy, they freeze, and then toy
broken, they claw at each other before falling away to
the floor like shattered pieces.

Run. Hide. I can't run. I can't hide. Everybody is out
to get me, they're out to get the ones I love, the one thing
I love. It's a war out there. It's like 'Nam. I remember.
This baby ran up to us. One of them with a piece of fruit
in her hand and a bomb in the other. And before she got
to me, that little one, that bomb blew up and her hand
went with it.

Brett looked at his empty hand as if it could be hers and
yet, his other hand, holding the gun, it *never . . . never
wavered.*

I saw that look on her face. She didn't know. I knew
then that she didn't know. They used her . . . understand . . . used her the way we were being used to keep
the war going . . . Her innocence was being used, just like
ours. Never was she wrong in that war. Just like us soldiers. Never were we wrong, fighting for what felt like
was good and right. All I want is to protect her . . . or is
it Mandy? No, it's Mandy. I want to save Mandy, my little
girl. I just want her to be safe, and happy. Like when we
used to go to this old boathouse to fish . . . There was a
little park nearby too. I'd take Mandy and put her on the
swings and on the slides. We were so happy then.

Brett backed away from the conference room where the

hostages were huddled together on the floor. Backing away . . . backing away . . . He turns into the camera, startled, as if suddenly caught naked. Reality back in his eyes.

Find Mandy or, God as my witness, I will blow this place up and may He have mercy.

Brett raised his hand to the lens and palmed the camera. It faded to black. Dump tape back to me live on set:

That dramatic videotape was shot just a short time ago. A handwritten note marked urgent was attached. That handwriting belonged to a Channel 8 cameraman being held hostage. He and everyone else in that bank should sit tight, because headway is being made.

Roll videotape. First shot is video of Mandy's bloody apartment, followed by an exterior of the county building where the victim worked.

Channel 8 News has learned the identity of the murder victim found inside Mandy's apartment. He is thirty-five-year-old Xavier Kurt, a parole officer with Cook County. Kurt is a ten-year veteran with the county and leaves behind a wife and two children.

B-roll of coroner's office followed by a photo of Kurt.

The county coroner's office performed an autopsy on the murder victim. The cause of death is recorded as a heart attack brought on by a violent beating, including several stab wounds with a screwdriver.

Chicago police are not sure what Kurt's relationship is to Mandy or her boyfriend Herc. Authorities say his law enforcement work may have led them to their apartment or he may have had an independent friendship with either one of them.

B-roll of Red Eye airplanes taking off.

What we do know is that Mandy worked for Red Eye Airlines until she was fired a few days ago. The airline refused to comment on her dismissal, referring Channel 8 to the union. The flight attendants' union also refused to comment but co-workers told us off camera that Mandy had been fired for some undisclosed misconduct or was given the right to quit.

Dump tape, come back to me live:

Georgia:
"The Channel 8 News team is now, along with police, following up with Mandy's friends to track down the people and places where she might seek refuge. If anyone out there has information on Mandy and her whereabouts PLEASE contact the Chicago police immediately. Lives are at stake. Mandy . . . if you or your friends are watching . . . come forward. Police promise to treat you fairly and promise to guarantee your safety. Pete?"
Pete:
"Georgia, what kind of trouble could Mandy be in?"
Georgia:
"There is some evidence that points to drug dealing. But Mandy's friends and her co-workers—all of whom

declined to be on camera—say she is a good person and a hard worker. Mandy's father has alleged that her boyfriend is the one involved with drugs . . . and Mandy may have unwittingly gotten caught up in some of his dealings. Whatever the case, authorities say they just want Mandy to come forward and get those hostages out of that bank safe and sound."

Pete:

"Thank you, Georgia."

Everyone was giving me my props on having a kick-butt story. But the clock was still ticking on my man Zeke and the other hostages.

That tape showed us two URGENT things. One, that Brett was beginning to lose it and that meant the hostages could be in danger. And two, that tensions were running high amongst the hostages themselves, which was another kind of danger all itself.

"Georgia!" an intern helping answer phones called out. "We got something."

He came rushing over and we all huddled in to hear what he had to say. "Got a call from a lady who works at a pizza parlor. Says a couple that looks like Herc and Mandy came in there a couple of nights ago to eat."

"Where?"

"Best's Pizza on Sixty-third and Ashland. She thinks she might know where they are. But she'll only talk to you—said something about wanting a reward. I told her—"

Paulie rudely interrupted. "Journalism 101, kid. We don't pay for freaking stories. That's the quickest way to ruin your rep and make some liars rich 'cause they'll say anything for a few bucks and a few minutes of fame."

"I know better. I told her we don't pay for stories BUT that the bank might give her a reward if this tip led to the end of the standoff."

I gave my man a high-five. "Great. What's the woman's name?"

"Lucy Winslow. Her shift is over in an hour. Can you catch her?"

Choke grabbed his face with both hands and moaned something in Spanish.

"What?" I asked.

Choke said, "If we gotta hurry, then that means Paulie keeps driving." Choke crossed his eyes. *"That's too loco."*

Paulie grabbed him around the neck. "Yeah, my man. We're about to get fast and loose."

Or should we say—fast and Lucy?

Lucy Winslow was no dummy. She told us to meet her out back in the alley. She was a tiny woman, less than five feet tall, thick arms, mahogany brown, drawn-on eyebrows arched heavily, and a 'fro cut so low she almost appeared bald. She was in her fifties and had a squeaky voice like the maid in *Gone with the Wind*.

I started the conversation. "Where are they?"

"I'm not saying anything 'til we talk about my dough. How much is the reward?"

Money was first and foremost on this woman's mind, that's for sure. But there was something else on her mind too. She kept cutting her eyes at Choke.

Flirt that he was, Choke winked back at her and put on a sparkling smile. And she halfway smiled back 'TIL she reverted to the subject of money again. "How much money is that bank willing to come up with?"

I half lied and half told the truth. "I will personally

call the bank president and tell him that you deserve
some reward money for your help."

"Some?" Lucy said sticking her hands in the pockets of the white apron she was wearing. "What we talking? Two thou? A grand?"

"Whatever they're offering Lucy, it's more money
than you've got right now."

She stared at me.

"C'mon, Lucy."

"All right, sistah," she said. "But don't you let them
cheat me outta my money. Here." Lucy reached in her
pocket and pulled out a rumpled piece of paper with
tomato sauce on it.

The Video Cowboys looked over my shoulders. It
was a delivery order. "Who is Grover? And what has he
got to do with anything?"

"Grover is a regular customer; a retired guy. He
used to be a bricklayer. He had a shoeshine business too
that was just around the corner. A couple of weeks ago
Grover ate pizza with them people y'all been looking
for."

"So you think he knows where they are now?"

Lucy sneered. "Ain't no maybe. He just had a pizza
delivered an hour ago. He ordered a super instead of the
medium. Said to send a bunch of plates and napkins.
When the delivery boy got back, I asked if Grover was
with a white couple—and he said yeah. Hurry and y'all
should be able to catch 'em." Then Lucy added sarcastically. "And maybe get you a slice of pizza too."

Choke hugged Lucy then twirled her off her feet. *"Te
quiero . . ."*

I laughed. Choke has only known her for something

like what—about two seconds—and already he's telling her he loves her.

"*Te quiero . . . you fine thing you!*"

She smirked and tried to play it off but she clearly adored the spin. "You make a habit of picking up women you don't know, and just twirling them around like a ten-cent top?"

"*Just a fine one like you.*"

"When I get my money maybe you'll come back and help me party with some of it?"

Choke winked and blew her a kiss.

Paulie snorted. "Come on, Casanova. We gotta get Mandy."

"Wait," I said. "We need a plan. They're not just gonna open the door and welcome us with open arms."

I glanced up at Lucy. "You're our in."

"Aww naw. I'm not signing up for no more than I already done."

Choke gave her a squeeze. "C'mon Lucy. Hear what Georgia has to say. We're not gonna let nothing happen to you. *Nada.*"

After he coaxed a smile out of her, I told everyone my plan.

We didn't have far to go to get to the Woodlawn area. It was a straight shot. We were heading to Sixty-third and Cottage Grove. Woodlawn is on the bubble. It used to be super fine with ballrooms where men dressed in starched suits and women carried clutch purses with their white-gloved hands. The neighborhood took a nosedive in the '60s and kept plunging for the next twenty years or so BUT now is on the upswing. The Uni-

versity of Chicago is nearby and began buying up land—
that put the area in gold rush status.

Run-down graystones are being gutted and re-
habbed or torn down and replaced by upscale condo
complexes. Still, there are strips of resistance and the
poor who are trying to hang on to their living space fight
against rising property taxes.

I had Gunner take a roundabout way to where we
were headed for two reasons. One: I wanted Choke to get
his mind right because he was the linchpin of my plan.
Two: I wanted to pass by St. Gelasius Church for good
luck.

A distinguished Catholic church that closed down
in 2002, St. Gelasius was built in a beautiful Renaissance
revival style that features a colonial tower with arched
breezeways in each square tier. The tiers build upward to
form a steeple that in turn hoists a stone cross. And to
think, some folks want to tear it down—mainly because
that property is worth a mint as a place to build some
condos.

But God don't like ugly.

Those with memories AND who don't want others
to forget are fighting to protect the grand old saint with
landmark status. I focused on that cross as we drove by,
praying hard that my plan would work and that nothing
bad would happen to Zeke or anybody else inside that
bank. We headed up a few blocks toward a series of large
storefronts underneath the el tracks. That's where Grover's apartment was, right next to the shoeshine parlor.

"Best's Pizza!"

I watched as Choke banged on the door of the

apartment. It was a funny setup. According to Lucy, the apartment was another storefront that this guy Grover had bought. That's where he lived while renting shoe-shine booths to guys at his business next door. He was semiretired and only craved two things. One was being able to shoot next door to talk with the young fellahs AND TWO was pepperoni and anchovy pizza.

My plan was simple but smart.

If Herc and Mandy were hiding out like we thought, they weren't going to open the door unexpectedly for someone they didn't know. But they did know Best's Pizza. They had just ordered a pizza so WE KNEW they weren't going to be ordering again anytime soon.

That's where Lucy came in.

I had Lucy call Grover and tell him the deliveryman screwed up and forgot about this new promotion the pizza joint was running: a free six-pack of Pepsi with each super-size pizza ordered. She was sending a new guy over with the pop.

Choke got tapped to play the deliveryman. He grumped but there was no other way to go. It was a black and Hispanic neighborhood. Because Paulie and Gunner were white, they would get made right off the bat. I couldn't do it because I'm on air and might be recognized. That left Choke to put on Lucy's apron and drive the putt-putt four-cylinder delivery mobile around the corner for the acting job of his life.

Gunner's camera was juiced, loaded, and resting on his shoulder ready to catch all the action on videotape. Gunner and I were on the side of the building watching. We were ready to back up Choke on the front side while

Paulie was in the alley just in case they came bolting out the back.

"Forgot my pop, huh?" an older man said, opening the door. His hair was heavily permed and combed straight back. It was the dirty white color of sea salt. This was Grover. He had the weathered appearance of an outdoor workingman: deep-set eyes, sunburnt ears, and skin that was flat in tone but rugged-looking. Grover wore jeans and a T-shirt that were spotted with every color shoe polish imaginable. His arms were long and his hands huge with bulging knuckles. He reached for the six-pack of pop that Choke had stacked on top of a couple of pizza boxes.

Choke cupped the pops with his hand and turned away. He faked a broken Spanish accent. *"I not sure this right place."*

"This it. This it." Grover told him.

"I no sure. Better call."

"Man," Grover hissed. "Come on in here then. And tell Lucy FOR ME that for all this grief, my next pizza should be free!"

Choke went inside the apartment.

He was going to pretend to call back to the pizza joint. But in reality he would call us if he spotted Mandy and Herc inside. My new cell phone vibrated against my stomach. I answered and waited to hear the verdict from Choke.

"Yeah. At first I was not sure this right place. Now looking around, it's right place."

That was our cue. Gunner and I braced ourselves to barge through the front door when Grover opened it again to let Choke out.

"Hey, what's your name, man?" The door opened. "I'll ask for you in case they try to charge me for my next pizza.

Gunner and I rushed forward. "He's Choke. And I'm Georgia Barnett, Channel 8 News."

Grover's jaw sagged like a pair of loose drawers.

Behind him Mandy and Herc started running toward the back door.

"Wait!" Choke shoved Grover aside and we took off after them. Gunner followed, videotaping everything. "We just want to talk to you, Mandy!"

They burst through the back door.

Paulie grabbed Herc up high. Paulie is not a small man but Herc made him look like one of the seven dwarfs. *Dopey to be specific.* This boy Herc wasn't as tall as Paulie but he was built like crazy. He had a big chest and a short, thick neck. Schwarzenegger arms. Bulging thighs showed through his torn jeans. He carried Paulie three feet—and again Paulie ain't skinny—before Choke tackled him low. They began tussling all over the ground. Boys play rough.

But so do girls.

Mandy was dashing toward an old Caddie that was parked in the alley, her long, light brown hair flowing behind her as she ran. She was a small woman and fast. I tried to keep up, but the girl was wearing flatfoot sandals, the rugged, comfy, fashion no-no kind that you could probably climb Mount Everest in.

"Wait! I need your help!" I shouted. Think she slowed down? *Please. Mandy ran like she was my nappy-headed stepchild and I was trying to comb her hair.*

She made it to the Caddie. The window was down and she was reaching inside to pull up the doorknob.

"Mandy! You gotta come with me!"

She whipped around and stabbed me with a car key she had in her hand. Mandy caught me on the shoulder blade and my knee buckled on my right side as pain shot through the bone in my neck and around to my back. My arm ached something fierce and I grunted.

Mandy popped up the doorknob and jumped in the car. All I could think was, *No this heifer didn't stab me.*

With the arm that wasn't aching to high heaven, I reached inside that car and grabbed her by the hair and yanked. She screamed. *Uh-huh. Homegirl can dish it out but she sho' can't take it.* She strained and stuck the key in the ignition.

"Wait!" I shouted again. "We're not gonna hurt you!"

Mandy opened the car door and rammed it against my midsection. I let her hair go and stumbled back, winded.

"Leave me alone!" she shouted and cranked the car engine. The motor spurted and snarled, and the smell of gas filled my nostrils as my body fought to get air.

I lunged back toward the car.

I heard the tires screech and smelled charred rubber as I threw my body halfway inside and tried to reach the key. Mandy whipped her elbow up and half-caught me in the chin. I let go.

She hit the gas.

I slipped back and felt my feet drag a few inches. I caught the headrest and pulled myself up. Mandy was now tearing down the alley and I was hanging on for dear life.

In the future when I tell this story to my mama, my man Doug, and my twin, and in the *far, far-out future* when I tell this story to my children, I'm going to lie *like a cheatin' husband.*

This black woman is going to say that she rode that car like the black cowboys rode broncos. I'm going to say I wasn't scared, I didn't scream, and that I had a plan.

Yep. That's what I'm going to say.

But this is what really went down. I was yelling my head off for this crazy woman to stop the car. I was neither cop nor killer. Mandy didn't have a thing to fear from me. So why was she putting my life in danger?

I was holding on, arms aching, eyes bulging as the street ahead rode up and down, pitching in my line of vision. She went from the alley we were in to the next. She didn't even slow down to see if another car was coming or anything. It was reckless escapism.

Mandy yelled, "Let go!"

Let go? Either she's a fool or she thinks I am.

How can I let go? She had to be going forty miles an hour. I'd be falling on concrete, NOT carpet. And Chicago concrete too. Hardened by harsh winters: that's tough stuff y'all. I'd bust my dome open for sure not to mention scar myself up from head to toe. So I clenched my teeth and HELD ON.

"Let go!"

I shouted back, "Slow down!"

We shot through the next alley.

Right about now my grip was feeling weak. Adrenaline was pumping in my body, though, driving my heartbeat like a black college drum line. I could hear it in my head and feel it against the walls of my chest.

Mandy hung a right out of this alley onto the street and I lost my shoes. My expensive shoes. My favorite pair of shoes. I love my shoes. I'm thinking if I live, I'm gonna kick Mandy's butt wearing my SECOND-FAVOR-ITE pair of shoes.

We went faster and faster.

All I saw was a blur of color, shiny metal. Those had to be parked cars. The wind filled my ears. My eyes started to lose focus from fatigue.

"Slow down!" I shouted. "Just slow down!"

Mandy swerved to miss a double-parked car and I almost threw up. She FINALLY put a little pressure on the brakes when she saw the traffic up ahead. I took that chance to pull myself back in the car. As soon as she slowed down, I pulled UP and IN with all my might and sat damn near in her lap between her upper torso and the steering wheel. The car swerved and suddenly we heard this horn blaring and people screaming.

We went right toward the curb and a storefront. I saw something that said "Mattress City," BEFORE the car hit the curb and bounced up. I went tumbling off the Caddie and landed up against a stack of mattresses piled against the building. My momentum made the mat-tresses come sliding down with me while the storefront window shattered and the car's brakes whistled.

BUT THIS IS NOT A BUPPIE MOBILE; *this is your daddy's Caddie.*

The front of that car was barely dented. Steel bumpers and the car was twice as long as my BMW. It took that hit like, "Say what?" Mandy opened the door, got out, and began slowly staggering down the street.

I couldn't get up to go after her; one, I had lost my shoes and two I had lost my wind. Now add three, I'd landed funny. My legs were spread wide open and were hung up against the wall as I lay on a mattress flat on the ground. Some young cat came over. He was grungy from head to toe and had the nerve to say, *"Aww girl. You landed just how I like it."*

Nasty D-O-G.

I was a wreck. My arms were numb from hanging on to that car for so long. My adrenaline ran out and I was paralyzed with fatigue.

My brain wasn't, though. It was more animated than a Disney cartoon.

Thank God I survived. Were Paulie and Choke able to hold Herc? If they were, would he tell us why the parole officer was murdered? Who were they hiding from? Where was Mandy going now that Herc was likely out of the picture? Could we find her in time to save Zeke and the bank hostages?

17

Gunner pulled up in the TV news truck shortly after I got enough strength to sit up. He swung my arm over his shoulder and stood me on my feet.

"Where are your shoes?"

"Couple of miles back, on the boulevard I think."

"You all right? Want me to call an ambulance?"

"I don't have time to be sick, Gunner. We've got to find Mandy. Did y'all hang on to Herc?"

"Yeah and it wasn't easy, Georgia."

"Please. It COULDN'T have been any rougher than what I had to put up with. I got the worst of it, honestly. Man I've been whipped around, whipped around, and whipped around some more."

"Take it easy a minute, Georgia. Just take it easy. All right?"

"How can I? We gotta help Zeke. Time is running out, Gunner."

"When was the last time you got carried over a puddle?" He swept me off my feet. "Upsie-daisy." Then Gunner walked to the van and asked a kid to slide open the panel door. He gently laid me down before grabbing a blanket and cradling it under my head. Gunner opened a Thermos full of water and soaked a T-shirt that was folded beneath the passenger seat. He laid the cold compress across my brow. Then Gunner got in on the driver's side and slowly pulled away.

Either it was the slow motion of the van OR the cold compress on my forehead OR the relief that I wasn't gonna wind up being trace evidence in the street next to some oil splat that leaked from a putt-putt stopped at a red light. It was something AMONG THE ABOVE or ALL OF THE ABOVE—whatever—I was out, as in *unconscious.*

When I woke up I was still inside the van, but I could hear men talking loudly. *My men.* The Video Cowboys.

Paulie: "This knothead is heavy, ain't he?"

Gunner: "Didn't you know muscle weighs more than fat?"

Paulie: "Who do I look like, Jenny Craig or somebody? Naw I didn't."

Choke: "Sit him down in the *silla.*"

Paulie: "Right. I'll cuff his hands behind him."

I leaned up and opened the van door. We were inside some type of a garage. I could smell oil. The van was parked almost against the wall. On the other side of the room there were a bunch of boxes stacked from the floor to the ceiling. Herc was knocked out, sitting in a folding chair. The Video Cowboys were now squatting on boxes.

What's the deal, I thought. Then I started firing off questions at them.

"Guys, where are we?"

"How'd you rest, Sleeping Beauty?" was Gunner's answer.

"Guys, no jokes. Where are we? And what's with Herc and the cuffs?"

Choke explained, "This used to be a tire shop but my baby sister Allie rents it out. She's got a mail-order company: just a little side business. She stores her goods here. I help her unload boxes sometimes so I pocket a key."

"But why are we here?"

Paulie thumbed toward Herc. "We needed to get some answers outta this man . . ."

"Pronto," Choke interjected.

". . . and we needed a quiet place . . ."

"Aquí . . ."

Paulie nodded at Choke. "And HERE was close, Georgia."

"But we gotta take him to the police."

Paulie assured me, "And we will AFTER we talk to him first. 'Cause if the cops get ahold of him, he's liable to LAWYER UP and CLAM UP. Then what, huh? Then where will Zeke and the hostages be?"

I checked out the hardware on Herc's wrists. "Where'd you get handcuffs?"

Choke said, "Outta one of the boxes."

"What kind of a business does your sister have?"

"She sells feminine products."

"Since WHEN are handcuffs a feminine product?"

Choke gave up the goods. "When it's the sex toy business."

"Ohhhh God!" Paulie laughed, rocking back on his box.

"Careful." Then Choke wagged his finger.

"C'mon! What?!" Paulie said, bouncing on the box some more.

"*No estoy jugando* . . . I'm not playing. That box you're sitting on is full of vibrators, Paulie. Keep bouncing. You might get one where the sun don't shine."

The Video Cowboys laughed.

Herc started to come around. He moaned.

I told the Video Cowboys, "I don't EVEN wanna know *how he got knocked out.*"

"Or how I got my elbows all scratched up!" Paulie huffed. "Or how Choke got that tomato-colored ear. This guy was a RAGING BULL."

Herc was trying to focus: "What? Where am I?" He looked around. "Who are you guys?" Then he saw me. "You're Georgia Barnett." He looked at Gunner. "That guy had a camera and he was with you." Herc then yanked on his wrists. "Who cuffed me?"

"I did," Paulie said stone-faced.

"Did you read me my rights?" Herc yanked at the cuffs. "I don't remember him reading me my rights. You got this cop on film giving me my rights? All I remember is him jumping me in the alley."

Herc assumed Paulie was a police officer. He thought this was some kind of a ride-along deal like the television show, COPS.

Paulie winked at us. "Don't worry about your rights.

Just tell the lady what she wants to know and we'll deal with charges later."

I started talking fast. "We need to know where Mandy is. Did you both know about her dad and the hostages he's holding at the bank?"

Herc acted deaf.

HOMEBOY WAS TRYING TO PLAY ME. *So I yelled. "Herc!"*

He yanked on the cuffs. "We know. We know."

"Then why didn't Mandy come forward and do something about it?"

"And get wasted?"

"Wasted?" I repeated. "By who?"

"By people who can get it done, lady. What? You thought we were playing hide-and-seek for fun or something?"

I leaned into Herc. "Look. We've got to find Mandy. Her father has a bank full of hostages at gunpoint. He's threatening to blow up the place unless he knows Mandy is safe and sound. And I've got a heck of a good friend in there and I don't wanna lose him."

"I'm sorry her old man is crazy. But I like life. Anywhere she might be hiding, THEY might be looking."

Herc was making me nuts. "Well if you're THAT scared, why didn't you just go—leave the city, the country for that matter. Mandy is a flight attendant. She could have arranged it."

"She wouldn't go 'til she knew her father was okay. She loves him too much. We were going to go pull him out of the hospital but he left on his own. His mind ain't right. So he's looking for us and we're looking for him.

Meanwhile THEY thought we had yanked him and figured we were about to bolt and all hell broke loose."

That answer made me soften somewhat. "So you
hung with Mandy, trying to help her find her dad?"

"I did it BECAUSE I care about her. But I can't
hang no more, lady. Look, I been straight with you guys.
Get this cop to turn me loose, huh? Give me a chance to
run, huh lady?"

"Your best chance is helping us find Mandy, then
we'll try to help you."

"Think, wouldya? If I take you to places Mandy
might be, THEY'LL be looking in those same places and
I KNOW I'll be a dead man walking then for sure."

Paulie webbed his end fingers together, then made a
gun out of his thumbs and index fingers. He pointed that
flesh gun straight at Herc. "So it's clear that THEY have
something to do with the drug thing you had going—"

"How do you know it was me and not her? Huh?"

"Maybe," Paulie deduced, "because it was your mug
on a wanted poster that her father held up. Evidently
you're a bad boy."

"I ain't a saint. But I love Mandy. Just give me a
chance to get away. This is a small-time collar for you.
C'mon."

Paulie asked, "Answer me this. You ever throw
Mandy ah beating?"

"What? Man please. Look at me. I lay a hand on
Mandy as little as she is, I'd hurt her something serious.
That ain't me."

"No." Gunner jumped in. "How's about drug dealing?"

"Listen, I'll give it to you guys straight. I started out

doing a little harmless stuff. Bodybuilding. Training people. Took a few steroids to get my bod right and started selling some myself in the gym. That's all. Nothing to write a script for *Law & Order* about, get me?"

Paulie pursued. "Peddling steroids shouldn't hang a death threat over your head, Herc. So how'd you go from steroids to the big time?"

"I'm not admitting nothing *especially to a cop.*"

I drew Herc's attention to me. "What's to admit? We already know you're dealing big-time."

Paulie grunted. "Yeah. There was a dead parole officer on Mandy's floor. And your friend out at Midway? He almost bought it too—if it weren't for Georgia here saving his butt."

Herc looked at me. "He okay?"

"Better than you. He's in protective custody."

"You're playing me." Herc raised an eyebrow. "Really?"

"Yeah, really. He's safe at the Wings Motel out by Midway. So don't worry about your buddy. Worry about you. We can help if you'd just tell us what the deal is."

Herc glanced down at the floor and said nothing.

Paulie badgered him. "Look at him, wouldya? A two-bit punk pushing drugs and robbing women at gunpoint." Paulie grabbed a fistful of Herc's hair and yanked his face to the right so they would be eyeball to eyeball. "That's you, right?"

"I ain't admitting to nothing. But hypothetically, sometimes people do a robbery when money is light. They're desperate. But they don't hurt nobody, see. So it's not so bad. Speaking hypothetically. No harm makes it a small beef. Everybody's hip to that."

Paulie let his hair go. "You stuck a gun in some-body's face and scared them half to death; they probably can't sleep, but who cares, huh Herc?"

"Since we're talking, let's talk the talk. Wasn't no bloodshed. No laying on of hands. And we all know that there are guys out there who like to rob people then beat or kill them just for the thrill of it."

I knew how to play good cop.

"Yeah, I agree. But wrong is wrong. Herc, listen. You're running. You want to keep on running forever? It's obvious these people you're talking about are big-time. The police can put you in protective custody, but you'll have to come clean about this drug mess you're in."

"I'm not admitting to nothing. I got rights."

Paulie leaned forward, elbows on his knees, matter-of-fact. "You got the right to go to county jail where you'll be the new Homecoming Queen. *Hypothetically speaking.*"

Herc swallowed. He paused for a while before turn-ing to Paulie. "If I say I know where Mandy is, what's in it for me? Can you get me some kind of a deal? For co-operating? You can swing that? You being a cop and all? Does there need to be a lawyer here?"

Now right here I was starting to feel bad, lying to this guy. But what choice did we have?

Paulie crossed his heart. "I'll talk to the state's attor-ney myself, kid. Swear to Mother Mary."

A loud creaking sound drew our attention to the garage door. Slowly it opened and a pretty woman walked in. She had a clipboard in her hand. She stopped and stared at us.

"Vicente? Paulie? Gunner? What are you doing here?" she asked. This was obviously Choke's baby sister Allie. They shared the same features. Nose. Mouth. Same brilliant black eyes: plus Allie had curly black hair that fell past her shoulders. She had a booming voice too. "How come that man is handcuffed? ¿Qué pasa?"

Choke rushed toward her. "Nothing, sis. I'll explain later."

"But I've got to take inventory. This is my business; you can't just push me out!"

Choke was trying to lead her to the door while she was trying to turn around to see what was going on.

Herc yelled, "This is your place? Good. That's right lady: make 'em get off your property. You got rights. So what, one of them is a cop. You've got rights."

"Who's a cop? They're a bunch of cameramen. Journalists. Vicente, what's he talking about?"

"Out out!" Choke pushed his sister through the door and went outside behind her.

"You lying bastards!" Herc growled and then charged—chair and all—at Paulie. Paulie swerved left like a matador and Herc's shoulder went crashing into a stack of boxes. The containers at the top came tumbling down with a thud. Herc whipped around again and the wooden folding chair snapped between his cuffed arms and his bulging back.

Gunner grabbed Herc by the neck and pulled him down. He put a sleeper hold on him and Herc kicked his legs like a wounded mule. His pant legs rode up his calves. Herc began to lose consciousness; his whirling legs began to slow and finally stop.

Choke came back in, "Hey, what happened?"

Gunner stood up, letting Herc slip to the ground still unconscious. "When he realized that Paulie's no cop and it's a bunch of Video Cowboys giving him the third degree, he snapped. Wouldn't you?"

"Allie is outside going *loco* too. She says she doesn't want any trouble. She wants us to call the cops and tell them to come get this guy."

Paulie nodded. "Might as well. Nothing else we can get out of him."

Choke swore in Spanish. "But we still don't know where Mandy is and time is running out."

Gunner looked down at Herc. He saw something and leaned in closer. He yanked up Herc's pant leg. "You guys see what I see?"

We leaned in closer. On the back of Herc's leg the hair had been shaved off. A key was taped to his calf.

Gunner ripped off the tape and grabbed the key. "Wonder what this leads to?"

Paulie said, "You better pray it leads us to a break."

My grandmother told me, *If you worry, don't pray. If you pray, then don't worry.* So I prayed and we made our next move.

After I called Captain Carey and told him where they could find Herc, we examined our one clue.

A key BUT a key with writing: "Republic Lock Box Co. #313." Republic Lock Box Company was located on the near north side, about two miles away from Mandy's apartment. It rented safety-deposit boxes like the banks, except for a lot less money. It was a large warehouse with hundreds of lockboxes built into the wall. There were dozens of cameras all over the place AND a couple of security guards.

When you went in, there was a check-in desk where you were supposed to show the clerk a state ID. The clerk would look up your box number and check your key to make sure that it matched. THEN and ONLY THEN were you allowed back.

Problem No. 1: we didn't have a state ID. Problem No. 2: we had to get to the lockbox before the cops found out we took the key.

How were we going to get the clerk to allow us in to get to the lockbox? A camera is a powerful weapon. It can make the meanest people nice and the nicest people mean. It can make the fearless fearful and the courageous cowardly. But most of all, it can make people do the darndest things just to be on TV.

"Hi, I'm Georgia Barnett. Channel 8 News."

The woman behind the desk was young, I'd say on the mature side of eighteen and just shy of twenty-five. She had a short haircut, black with light brown highlights, kind of an artsy look. Two earrings in each ear; large eyes. A baby blue crewneck T-shirt and hip-hugger, embroidered jeans. She had copper bangles on her right arm. When she heard what I said and looked up and saw the camera, she became overjoyed.

"Oh my God. TV."

"We're here to do a story on your company."

Her smile disappeared. "Is something wrong? Maybe I should call Mr. Braxton, the manager."

Playah playah Choke was running camera this time. He touched her hand as she reached for the phone. "Nothing's wrong. Don't call him. Our viewers would much rather see a pretty girl like you."

She laughed, her eyes twinkling. "Okay. I'm Kellie by the way."

Got a name, run the game. "Kellie, one of our cameramen is a customer of yours and he gave us his lockbox key. We want to show our audience how sturdy the boxes are and how much you can store in them."

"Well, *where's he?*"

Choke said, "Couldn't make it. There's a bank robbery going down on the other side of town and he had to go cover it."

"Well," Kellie bit her bottom lip. "We're not supposed to allow anyone in the box area unless the person proves they're the owner by showing a state ID."

"It'll be okay," I reassured her. "There's nothing wrong. We're doing a consumer story on ways that people can protect valuables outside of the home."

"Oh."

"Kellie, you heard on the news about the increase in home burglaries? And everybody knows that there's always the possibility of a house fire. So, we're showing our viewers ways to store and protect important documents outside the home."

"Like the lockbox," Kellie smiled. "Cool."

"Ever been on TV before?" Choke asked.

"No."

I told her, "Then this is your lucky day." *And a good turn of events for us too, I might add.*

The lockbox had three things in it. One was a jewelry box with a couple of expensive watches, ladies' and men's, and some other gold items, but nothing to break the bank. A couple of the rings had different initials on them.

"Probably stolen loot," Choke reasoned.

I picked up a small, empty wallet with a couple of pictures in it. Mandy and Herc at the beach. Then the two of them with their friend Steve at a street fair; looked like New Orleans.

Underneath the wallet, I found an ID with Herc's picture on it.

It was a work ID for the Cook County Juvenile Rehabilitation Complex. Herc was a guard at juvie jail. Weird. A man who is mixed up in drug dealing and street robberies is a guard at juvie jail? He's supposed to be upholding the law, not breaking it—right?

Choke took Kellie's hand and kissed it, "Thank you for your help."

He is a mess y'all. "Come on here Choke! We've gotta go!"

We jumped in the van and hightailed it over to the juvie jail to find out more information about Herc. While riding in the van, I got an idea. "Hey, where's the list of the dead P.O.'s parolees?"

Gunner reached under his seat and tossed it back to me.

"Thanks Gunner."

"Whatcha thinking?" he asked.

"Well, we just assumed that the dead P.O. had some kind of a hand in the drug dealing with Herc and Mandy. Maybe he was there about a parolee—somebody who had put their time in at the place."

Choke finished my thought. "And that would be how he knew Herc and sought him out?"

"Possibly," Paulie said.

I flipped through the list and scanned the names. It only listed names, addresses, stint of parole, and the last time the P.O. had contact. "Doesn't say where they were paroled from," I told the Video Cowboys. "Gunner, can your nephew tell us that?"

Gunner whipped out his cell phone and dialed his nephew. He spoke with him. "For all of them?" Gunner asked over his shoulder.

I nodded my head sheepishly. "Could he?"

Gunner asked him, then hung up. "He'll call back."

"Remind me to take my man Jeff to lunch, Gunner. He's been the bomb. Did he say how the people in the office were taking the murder?"

"Tough. Says it's blue, blue around there. Everybody's upset. If it's a parolee, heaven help all the other ones. They're gonna catch it for sure. You think a parolee is the connection?"

I shrugged. "That's all I can see. If we can figure out what the scam is, we'll have something to come at Herc with. With that ammo, Herc will probably give Mandy up."

Gunner turned around. "You think he knows where she is?"

"If you and a person you loved were running for your lives, wouldn't you brainstorm a plan or two?"

Now I know jail ain't supposed to be pretty. Grown-up jail ain't no joke. Jails for grown-ups like Joliet are a pit. County jail isn't much better either; it's a concrete hole. But we DO want to try and rehab our troubled youth, right? Not to sound like a bleeding heart who's soft on crime. That's not my voice. That's not my choice. *BUTahrah*, if you asked me, if these parents would get tough with their children when they're little, so many of them wouldn't end up in and out of jail, doing drugs, and other crimes. Feel me?

'Cause they need to know that juvie jail *ain't nothing nice either.*

There are bars on each and every window. Guards had TWO nightsticks: one on each hip. The rooms were small with a cot on each side and a toilet in the middle.

The door was solid steel with a square, no glass, but three bars close together. There was a common area where the kids could sit and watch TV, move around, but guards were on a high tier watching. There were some classrooms where you saw a handful of teens learning math and science.

The director spotted us immediately. To his credit, he knew the deal. The man was no dummy. Herc worked for him—he was going to have to do spin control. That was inevitable. So why not get in good with the reporter who would break the story first?

"This was Herc's wing," the director said, standing next to us on the tier above the row of rooms and open common area. "Never had a problem out of him. Always came to work on time. Seemed fair and courteous with the kids. I can't believe what he's mixed up in."

"How do you screen your applicants?" Gunner asked. "How thorough are the background checks?"

"I can show you his file. He checked clean. No record before he started working here in January 2000. We had a lot of retirees. Turnover here is bad too. The wages are low. It's thankless. And every now and then it gets a little dangerous."

"How?" Choke asked.

"Kid came at a guard with a fork the other day. Two more kids from rival gangs went at it with folding chairs." The director shrugged. "Ugly stuff but not unusual for the bunch we've got here."

"Did Herc befriend any of them? Could we talk to them?"

"That's out, Georgia. I can't let you talk to any of the

juvies, but all the men that Herc worked with are on this tier. I'll take you around and let you talk to them. No filming though."

We talked to four guards who worked regularly with Herc. Not one of them had a bad thing to say about the guy. The director wouldn't let us talk to the kids so we were at a dead end AGAIN.

We went back to the director's office, our lips and hearts dragging on the floor. Gunner's cell rang. "My nephew says that the P.O. had three kids that came from here."

The director settled into his chair. "Who? I'll pull their records. Can't let you see it but I can give you an idea if there's something there."

Gunner nodded, then told his nephew, "Shoot." He listened and then repeated the names. "First . . . there's Wayne Issacson."

The director wrote the name down on the pad. "I remember him. Smart mouth but not much to him."

"Calvin Kenner."

"He's one of my success stories. Turned his life around. He's doing well. He's got a stable job and living situation."

"And Patrelli Manotti the third."

The director dropped his pen.

I asked, "Is that *the* Manotti? The crime family Manotti?"

The director nodded.

Paulie said, "I hear that kid is as treacherous as his old man and grandpa."

The director nodded again.

"Geez," Paulie hissed.

Gunner thanked his nephew and hung up. "I've heard tales about the Manotti family, but all that stuff ain't true, is it Paulie?"

"Yeah, according to my father and my grandfather. Patrelli Manotti was a hit man for Al Capone. Back then the machine gun was the big new toy, only Manotti didn't like 'em. He said they were too loud; hurt his ears. In the old country, his people were butchers by trade. They started a business here when they came over and taught Manotti too. My grandfather worked for a competing butcher who got muscled out. Some honest guys and the gang just shut them down."

I noticed some animosity in Paulie's voice. *A little something-something personal slipped in.*

"The Manottis. Manotti's meat. They got big. They carved up veal and whatnot for the local stores; some of their cuts even got shipped to fancy restaurants out east, which was the only real way to make money in those days. So Manotti was Zorro with a knife. The family trade came in handy when he turned crooked and hooked up with Capone. Manotti would carve up his victims like a filet."

Gunner reached in his pocket for a smoke. "You're for real? Those stories are really true, Paulie?"

"And then some."

I threw in my two cents. "His son, Manotti Jr.— Manny—went on trial last year for running a bookie operation. He beat it. At least he's not a hit man."

Paulie laughed. "Word in the neighborhood is that Manny learned a tough lesson from his old man in the Al Capone days. His father would leave his bodies out like a calling card, bragging like. Building a rep. But my old man said that's how he got pinched. Each generation learns from the last, Georgia."

"So Manny didn't hang his dirty laundry out on the line?"

"So they say."

Choke asked, "What was his kid in for?"

"Trey Manotti?" the syllables dropped from the director's mouth. "He was in for drug dealing. And a nasty little son of a bitch he was too. When he got paroled I was glad to see him go, Georgia."

"When did he get sprung?"

"Summer of 2001, when he turned eighteen."

I figured. "So he was here while Herc was. Same tier?"

The director got up and went over to a file cabinet. He rifled through some folders, pulled one out, and looked. "Same tier. Maybe he's Herc's drug dealing connection. Herc never struck me as the scary type. But if there was ever someone to fear, it's ANYBODY named Manotti."

As soon as the director said that my cell phone went off. I looked at the number and told the Video Cowboys, "Clarice." Then I answered the call. I spoke loud so that the Video Cowboys would know what was going on. "Can we get back to the station to do a set piece?"

Paulie balled up his fist and threw a slow thrusting punch in the air.

I nodded. "Done deal."

Good afternoon everyone. I'm Georgia Barnett.
Right now at Area B Police Headquarters there's a

man who has been the subject of an all-out manhunt by the police and the media since an intense hostage stand-off unfolded this morning at Lake Michigan Bank. His name is Herc Quarterman. He's thirty-two years old and the boyfriend of Mandy Mitchell, whose father is holding the hostages at gunpoint and claims to have a homemade bomb. Channel 8 News has exclusive proof that Mandy is alive and well.

Video changes to Choke chasing Mandy and Herc out of the back way of the storefront apartment next to the shoeshine parlor.

(Natural sound, Mandy yelling "Run! Run!")
The Channel 8 News team was able to track Mandy and Herc down. They'd been holed up in a small south-west side apartment. The video has been slowed but you can clearly see that Mandy is fine . . .

B-roll of Mandy jumping in the Caddie; she takes off, and I hang on.

She takes off in a car parked in the alley set up for a quick getaway. I managed to hang on to the fleeing car for several blocks but Mandy escaped, unharmed.

Video changes to Herc in cuffs being put in a police car. Followed by exteriors of the Cook County Juvenile Rehabilitation Complex. Then cut to the police sketch that Brett held up in the bank.

Herc Quarterman was arrested. Quarterman worked

as a guard at the Cook County Juvenile Rehabilitation Complex and sources say he may have made a pact with insiders who are heavily connected with the Chicago mob and the drug trade. Right now Quarterman is being questioned by Chicago police about drug dealing, a string of robberies, AND OF COURSE the whereabouts of Mandy.

Dump tape and come back to me live at police HQ.

To Brett, whom I've been communicating with via videotape, I've now shown you proof that Mandy is alive. In return, you need to let at least one of the hostages go. Be fair, Brett. Show the world that you have compassion. Please. Meanwhile, we'll keep looking.

Pete?

I left the set and was met in the hallway by the Video Cowboys. Gunner winked. "Nice job. Think Brett'll listen?"

"God, I hope so, Gunner."

"Georgia!" an intern yelled.

"I don't know fellas. Where do we go from here?"

"Georgia! Phone."

I was grouchy. "Shoot it to voice mail. I don't have time to chitchat."

"Oh, you wanna take this call."

"Why?"

19

Because it was Mandy.

The Mandy. The slick chick who had managed to elude the cops and us too. Barely. The same one who had me hanging on to her car, dragging me down the street like a coattail caught in the door.

That Mandy.

She called on the tip hotline. We checked the caller ID we had on it. The device read: Unlisted.

"Mandy?"

"Yeah."

"Listen. We've been looking for you. We're not trying to hurt you. Your father—"

"My father's in trouble."

"And only you can help him."

"Get him his meds. He's not taking his prescription. Check with Callahan's, the pharmacy on Polk. Right off the expressway on the corner. I just put a prescription in for him."

I grabbed a pen and scribbled down the drugstore and the address. Then I wrote: CALL POLICE. She must still be in that area.

Clarice scrambled to the phone. I tried to keep Mandy on the line. I had to keep her on the line and in the vicinity of the store.

"You sound scared, Mandy."

"I am scared."

"I know you're tired of running, girl."

She huffed into the phone: her breath was quick and grunting.

"Listen Mandy, the police can protect you and Herc—"

Mandy snorted. "Yeah? I don't trust cops. Never have. Cops. Social workers. County doctors. They're all the same. They don't care about nobody. They don't give a damn about families and their kids and how they feel. They follow rules. Stupid rules and try to make people live their lives out of a manual. We don't live like that. Not me. Not my dad."

"I'll come get you, Mandy. Where are you?"

"Are you listening? Does ANYBODY listen?"

"Mandy, I'm listening. I am."

"Then hear this. We're there for each other. We're family. Just get my daddy his meds."

"But he's talking about killing people, Mandy."

"Just get him the medicine!!"

Then she hung up.

The Video Cowboys and everyone else in the newsroom had been hanging on my every word.

I squeezed the receiver and slammed it down. "She's gone. Let's go."

"To the drugstore?" Gunner asked.

"Yeah. She just put a prescription in for her dad. She was probably calling from a pay phone around there. I heard street noises."

We hightailed it to our truck and shot over to Callahan's. It was a small store that the Callahan family opened at the turn of the twentieth century. Like many other neighborhood one-stop shopping places, it was now being forced out by all the big boys like Walgreens, Target, and Wal-Mart.

Dropping a dime on Mandy wasn't nothin' but a word; cop cars were all over the place. They were cruising through the streets. I had Clarice on the phone. "The cops find anything? I see they're out here in full force."

"Nope. My sources say nothing yet."

We pulled up to the drugstore and parked out front. The Video Cowboys and I ran inside. We headed straight for the back. I spotted the detective right away: bushy hair, clean-shaven face, dark blue suit. He was tapping his notepad with his pen as he asked the pharmacist questions.

The pharmacist was lanky, young, and seriously starched. He had on a crisp white shirt and lab coat. His name tag said "Ted."

"Detective. I'm Georgia Barnett. Channel 8 News. And this is my crew." I pointed to the Video Cowboys. "I called in the tip about Mandy."

He nodded. "I heard."

"What can you give me?"

He gave me a blank stare.

"C'mon. I phoned it in. Everybody knows I'm trying to help."

"Off the record?"

I nodded.

"She was here. We've got squads searching the area for her. This is the pharmacist who took the prescription from her. He says she used to come in all the time when she lived around here a few years ago."

"I didn't know—" Ted said, wiping his brow. "If I'd known, I would have tried to keep her here or snuck to the back and called the police. But we don't get any news around here. No TV. No radio. Nothing."

Guilt was rattling him like a tin can.

The detective said to me, "There's nothing here."

"What about the prescription?" Gunner asked.

The eager pharmacist volunteered. "We're filling it."

I jumped at an opportunity. "We can take it to him."

"No dice," the detective scoffed. "Captain Carey already got the word from Whelk. I'm taking it to the S.W.A.T. team. They're going to use it as a bargaining chip; try to trade it for a couple of hostages."

Paulie warned, "Crap . . . you're gonna tick the guy off."

The detective groused. "Well he's ticked us off."

I tried to talk to the pharmacist. "Sir—"

The detective stepped between us. "That's all the juice you get here. Sorry. No interviews."

That was that. So we left.

Outside, the phone in our news truck rang. "Yeah?" I answered.

It was Clarice. "They've saturated the area and STILL no sign of Mandy. They found one witness who said she thought Mandy got in a cab but she couldn't remember what kind of cab. It was an elderly lady, sweet thing but she can't seem to even remember what color the cab was. Looks like another dead end, girlfriend."

Man, can a sister get a break? "Okay Clarice. Keep us posted. I'll let you know our next move." I thought, then mumbled, "Let's reverse it."

"*¿Qué?*" Choke prodded.

"Let's switch gears. Instead of trying to find Mandy, let's look for Manotti. He's after her, right? It's our best-case scenario. We find him he might lead us to her; if we just get him, the threat to Mandy is gone and maybe that'll be enough to get Herc to tell us where she's hiding."

Gunner said, "Yeah. Sounds good. Fellas?"

Everyone agreed with me. "Good, but let's not go off hunting down a mob boy with holes in our drawers. We need to know all we can about the Manotti crime family. Let's head back to the station. Clarice can pull some of the old stories we've done on them."

Back at the station, an intern met us in a screening room with an armload of tapes. On each and every last one of them was a story about SOMEBODY named Manotti or SOMEBODY connected to the family.

Clarice shook her head. "Look at all that tape. We oughta be working for the History Channel."

"Okay," I said, glancing over the log-in sheet that gave a brief description about what was on each file tape. "How about this one. It's an anniversary piece on the St. Valentine's Day Massacre when Capone had all those guys from a rival gang machine-gunned to death in a garage. It covers a history of Chicago's mob families . . . including the Manottis. Let's look at that for background."

We sat and watched the special report that had aired during February sweeps. The report was put together by the station's veteran crime reporter, who had since retired. We fast-forwarded to the part on the Manottis, *particularly Manny*. A reporter told the story:

Manny Manotti is one of the few crime figures today whose heritage can be traced all the way back to the days of Al Capone. His father Patrelli Manotti was a vicious hit man for Al Capone. His trademark was a filet knife that he used to partially skin his victims. It was a trademark that led to his arrest and made it easy for police to track which mob hits were actually his handiwork. Patrelli was convicted on three counts of murder and died in prison.

His son Manny was sixteen at the time. He found an unsavory set of father figures at this wholesale billiard supply store in Chicago's Bridgeport neighborhood. The front half of the building is a pool hall and social club frequented by connected and made men only. It remains open to this day and insiders say it still boasts the same criminal clientele.

Manny Manotti spurned the hit man role in mob life for that of a lower-key and very lucrative sports betting operation. Police estimate that the Chicago racket brings in more than three million dollars a year. Manotti has been arrested several times in connection with the operation but has avoided conviction every time INCLUDING last year.

Manny is shown here coming out of court, all smiles, with his family after being found not guilty. His son Patrelli Manotti the third, Trey, is at his side, himself already no stranger to courts and criminal charges. He has been arrested on several misdemeanors and is allegedly cutting his teeth on the drug trade here in the city.

The apples may not fall far from the Manotti tree.

End of tape.

I turned to Paulie. "Can you get us into that social club with the good old boys?"

Paulie smiled. "Yeah. No problem. But we gotta go in thumping our chests 'cause these are not namby-pamby types of folks. They respect straight shooters. Now, I can get you audiences with the right people, Georgia. But I gotta lead. I know when to push. I know when to backpedal."

"I'll follow your lead. I really don't have a smidgen of a problem with letting you be the chief while I play the role of the Indian."

"Good. 'Cause I still have family in the old neighborhood. I don't wanna have to look under my car hood the next time I go to my aunt's for Sunday dinner."

"Paulie," I said, "we're not about to lose you, OR Zeke either for that matter. Mob boys or not, let's go get 'em."

And the Jackson Five sang, *"Get it together or leave it alone."* And we weren't about to leave it alone, so we had it all together when we went to the Billiard Club.

Paulie told Gunner, "Shoot exteriors of the place from across the street. You and Choke stay out here in the van and do the videotaping."

"Why?" Gunner asked.

"'Cause if they see that camera, they'll freak and I don't feel like getting my chops busted, Gunner."

"Won't they be MORE CAUTIOUS *if they see* the camera?"

"No. They'll think I'm ambushing them. They know I work in TV news but I never ambushed anybody. Georgia coming in with me will let them know that I'm on official business and to be cool. Taking Choke would look like I'm scared or expecting trouble. That's why he stays with you, Gunner."

We all agreed.

"Georgia, let's roll."

We walked into the Billiard Club, which was nothing to write home about. It was a plain, sandy-colored brick building with a large window in front. A rectangular sign, white background, black flat paint formed the lettering across the front. The sign was mounted on the top half of the building. Bulb lights, which flashed primary colors, were strung around the sign.

When we opened the door, the banging of bass voices giving each other the business hung heavy in the air. The volume dropped, as well as a few eyes, when they saw us walk in.

Paulie let it fly. "Greeting chumps! The best pool hustler in town is here!"

There were about five guys who looked to be senior citizens and about four more in their late forties. One young man who couldn't have been more than twenty-one was leaning against the wall fiercely eyeing us. Two other guys grabbed their coats and walked right past us without saying a mumbling word, not even excuse me. Paulie sniffed under his arms before parroting a popular TV commercial. "That's the reason why, you need Soft and Dry."

All the old guys got tickled. One asked, "What brings you around here, Paulie? Official business I see." He nodded toward me. "This one here? She's prettier in person than on TV."

"Georgia, that's Melvin Mantegna. Mellow for short. The sweetest-talking Italian on the southwest side."

He had a gray Dobbs hat, red band, and feather. Grey cotton shirt, slacks, and patent-leather shoes. I smiled at him. "My pleasure."

Mellow tipped his hat.

"Game of pool, Mellow?"

"Why not?"

I pulled Paulie's coat. "We don't have time for that."

He whispered back, "Let me roll with this." Paulie asked Mellow, "I break?"

"No. I got a bum ticker and my *gooma* just passed. You're strong as a Mack truck and you walked in here with a pretty woman. Your luck is better than mine, son. That's for sure. I'll break."

Paulie pulled a Jim Carrey face and made us laugh. But one person in the room didn't find it quite so funny.

The young twenty-something walked to the pool rack and grabbed a stick. "It's my game, Mellow." A cigarette was dangling out of his mouth. He was trying hard to appear seasoned. "Me and you, we had next."

Paulie raised his eyebrows. "It won't take long. I'm just here for a few minutes and Mellow always lets me win."

"Yeah, well, I've been waiting and I got business so it's my go."

Mellow didn't say a word. Neither did any of the other men inside. Why were they letting this kid try and punk Paulie? Was he doing it on their say-so? Or was this on his own, in an effort to strut like a peacock?

Paulie grabbed a stick and stepped back. "Why don't we let Mellow set up a trick shot and whoever sinks it plays next?"

Mellow offered up. "Good idea."

He grabbed the balls and set up a trick double bank shot. The kid missed and Paulie made it with ease.

"Sorry kid." Paulie started to rack 'em.

"An old fart like you can pull off all the tricks, huh?" The wannabe made man was posturing for his seasoned audience. "Where'd you learn that one? Back in the '40s?"

"Geez," Paulie laughed. "I'm not that old. But if you wanna know *exactly* how old I am, ask your mother. She gave me my first taste on my fourteenth birthday."

Aww naw. Now see. No matter what culture it is . . . black, white, Hispanic, or Asian . . . whatever . . . talking about somebody's mama means IT'S ON . . . *for real.*

The kid swung his pool stick. Paulie ducked and then slammed his fist into the young man's rib cage. The kid threw a weak punch as he was doubling over. Paulie grabbed the kid's wrist, slammed his hand on the green carpet of the pool table, and held it there while grabbing the eight ball, smashing it down on the back of the kid's knuckles. The kid screamed in pain.

"Another old trick," Paulie said. "Hurts like the devil, don't it?"

None of the old guards standing around uttered a word. That's when I knew. Paulie had *dap, props, kudos, or history*—WHATEVER—with the people in this room, and although I was sure that he wasn't mobbed up, he was damn sure respected.

Mellow said, "You wanna take this out back, Paulie?"

Paulie leaned more weight on the kid's hand. The kid groaned louder, tears welling up in his eyes. "Yeah, let's." Paulie twisted the kid's arm behind his back and started walking toward a side door.

I started following Mellow out the back, but he turned and ordered, "This is no place for ladies." Then he glanced around the room at his crew. "Keep our guest entertained, fellas."

I wanted to holler at Paulie, don't leave me alone with all these strange men. These *seen-the-world men.* These *done-things-they're-afraid-to-tell-their-mamas men.*

But I didn't. Why not? Simple. Because I knew that if I went prissy in front of a bunch of *hard-jawed, block-heeled wiseguys* that I would NEVER be able to adequately cover ANYTHING in this world again. Word would get around. That's one thing that cops, reporters, and criminals have in common: your street rep can make or break you.

One of the older men came toward me. He had a wide-legged step aided by a mahogany, pearl-handled cane. He was grizzled around the eyes with turkey skin hanging beneath his chin, and beautiful silver hair.

I looked at him and he looked at me. I picked up the cue stick and said, "Eight ball. Rack 'em."

The other men chuckled but he went ahead and racked 'em. "Ladies first."

Like he was giving me a handicap. Hey, like my grandmama used to say, *If you see me fighting the bear don't help me, help the bear.* Ya know my people on my mother's side were a bunch of blues singers, right? Chitlin Circuit. Wooden floor. Turning on the air meant opening a window. Cover charge was a couple of quarters dropped into a sweat-stained hat. Those kinds of blues folks from yesteryear. When my twin Peaches and I were shorties, small enough to be sat on a pool table, we'd watch as my grandmama hustled up change during the day at a billiard parlor next to the blues joint where she sang at night. She taught us how to shoot too.

Now, when you're visiting somewhere you're supposed to have manners, supposed to be a lady. That's
according to the *black girl's guide to home training*. BUT-
AHRAH . . . Zeke was in trouble. The clock was ticking
on us finding Mandy. We had less than three hours to go.
Paulie was trying to get info out of some young punk out
back AND I was tired and running on high-octane hope.

I told myself, *later alligator* for manners and *after a
while crocodile* for being a lady. I wore that table out: sat
on the side with my hips curved up to the sky, leg hiked
up—THANK GOD I didn't have on a dress, otherwise all
those Soprano knockoffs would've seen gold *in them
there hills.*

I went to work. Twelve ball banked off the three,
into the side pocket. Ten ball straight down and back to
the corner pocket. By the time I cleared the table of all
my balls EXCEPT the dreaded eight ball, Paulie came
strutting through. The kid came and sat down in the corner with his head down. Mellow stopped and admired
the table from the corner. "Paulie," he said, "you ain't no
good. You brought a ringer down here to hustle us. She
wins, we'll never live it down."

I looked at the old man I was playing and his face
was blank. I saw his gnarled hands squeezed raw around
the pearl handle of the cane. What Mellow *really* meant
was *they would* never LET HIM live it down.

"Eight ball corner pocket." I drove the cue stick
high off the white ball making SURE that it drove the
eight ball forward into the pocket, while crawling right
in behind it.

"Scratch!" Paulie said, pleased. "Let's roll, Georgia."

I left the stick on the table and when I walked around my opponent I whispered, "Mercy mercy me, of all the luck."

When we got back outside, my heart was racing and my ears burned. I told Paulie, "Boy, don't you EVER leave me hanging like that again."

"What?"

I thought about how I was totally outnumbered. "I was at a disadvantage."

"YOU are NEVER at a disadvantage, kid." Paulie looped his arm around my shoulders and gave me a hug. "You done good in there."

Dog! And I wanted to be mad too! But he made me grin. "Thanks, Paulie. How'd you do with the kid? Get anything out of him about Trey Manotti?"

"Baby, I scored."

Apparently Kid W, as in wannabe, was tight with Trey Manotti and gave up the names of his friends and where they hung out. I was curious.

"Why give up the info? He has to have a gut and know that you're not a killer. He was THAT AFRAID of a beating from you, Paulie?"

"The beatin' wasn't it. He was bowing down 'cause he knew I'm in Mellow's good graces. Everyone in that room owes Mellow big-time. And Mellow hates the Manotti family from way back; their grandfathers had a thing like those hillbillies—the Hatfields and the Mc-Coys."

"Then why was the kid even there if he's cool with Trey Manotti?"

"His father and Mellow did time together in the

joint. There's still an unwritten rule that anytime one of them can jam up the other on the sly, they do, but there's been a truce for years."

"Now what, Paulie?"

"I've got a bunch of names and a few addresses. Do we roll the dice and hit an address? Or do we somehow weed this down? And if we decide to weed it down, how?"

Blessed are the flexible for they shall not get bent out of shape. We decided to weed it down. I've got a good friend who could help us. We got back in the truck with Gunner and Choke. They said they heard on the radio that the police had used a bullhorn to tell Brett that they would trade a hostage for his meds. Apparently he was ignoring them. What did they think? Just because the man was mentally challenged didn't mean he was stupid.

We turned our attention to the lonely-only clue we had: weeding down Paulie's bad-boy list. To that end, I had to call on one of my best girls. Her name is Sylvia. We sped over to her cop shop where she's a lieutenant. We went to the same high school and had our first taste of wine together behind the bleachers in the gym when we were juniors. Got sick as dogs drinking that mess. Come to find out Peaches, who we sent to get it 'cause she looked older than she was, bought the cheapest bottle of *chugalug* she could find and pocketed the remainder of our money. After some rest and recovery, we beat her down. *But God knows it took both of us to get the job done.* Sylvia's old-school voice refreshed me.

"Georgia. Only YOU can be in *as much mess* as you've been in today and STILL keep coming back for more." Sylvia was tall, big-boned, and on sight would seem intimidating to some people; but girlfriend was just confident. *I liked it in her.* Tall: she wore heels. Big-boned: she had her clothes fitted to accent those *River Niger hips.* Sylvia had a big laugh and a smile that went along with it, WHICH she showed to me now after I quickly introduced her to the Video Cowboys. "Okay, intros over. Let's get to work."

The Chicago Police Department was doing a good job fighting gang and organized crime. They had set up a special computer program that would access suspects' files quickly: giving last known addresses, their entire criminal record, nicknames, where they did time, mug shots, even the lead district attorney on the case IF it actually went to trial.

Sylvia took control. "Give me the names and we'll pull up their jacket. If anything looks remotely cute, I'll send a squad out to haul 'em in."

Sylvia had a cigarette hanging out of her mouth, the ash a mile long, glowing dusty amber gray. Choke inhaled and sounded like he was sucking all the air out of the office, NOT JUST the nicotine hurricane twisting from her cigarette into his nasal path. Sylvia and I cut our eyes at one another.

Sylvia didn't wanna be the reason that Choke tumbled off the nonsmoking wagon. She let the cigarette fall from her lips. Then I stomped it out on the crusty tile floor.

Choke cussed us in Spanish then swung into slang, 'cause he likes to hang out with the young honeys. "Y'all are hating on me."

That's when I saw it. When Choke said that and I looked down. I never noticed it before. Kinda like how you look for your keys and they're on the coffee table EVEN THOUGH you glanced there more than once. It was there all the time. The clue. The connect. The real break we'd be hoping, hustling, and waiting to say hallelujah about.

"Oh my God!"

"What?" Gunner said.

"On this parolee list? The one we got from your nephew Jeff? Look at this address. That's Mandy's address!"

"*Sí,*" Choke breathed. "But Mandy wasn't on parole. Neither was Herc."

My eyes followed the address line backward until I reached the name that I read out loud. "Michael S. Watson."

Sylvia said, "I'm gonna drop his name in."

I stood, not sat, waiting for the computer screen to pull up and display the info on Michael S. Watson. *Then it came.*

The mug shot on the left, the primary info on the right. Nobody said a mumbling word but Sylvia sensed something was up just from the look on our faces as the picture completed itself entirely.

She poked at us. "What? What?"

Paulie growled, "That lying little punk."

Choke whined, "We saved him too!"

Gunner laughed sarcastically. "He played us, didn't he, Georgia?"

Like my twin sister Peaches sings in one of her blues ballads, I was mad as a whore in a girdle. "Yeah he played us but the PLAYAH is about to get some payback."

Sylvia was confused. "What are you guys talking about? You know this guy?"

Paulie tapped the computer screen with his finger. "Michael S. Watson. Is Steve Watson. He obviously dropped the Michael for his bus-driving gig out at Midway Airport. He's the one we were talking to when we got shot at. Georgia got some of Doug's boys to take him to one of those shady motels out by the airport to lay low. He SWORE he wasn't in on the drug game, just that he hung with Herc and Mandy. He let us think that the shooter was trying to scare us off the story."

Gunner said, "You know what I think now? I think maybe they were AFTER HIM all along, don't you?"

Choke laughed sarcastically. "One thing is clear. We know FOR SURE Steve knows more than he let on. *The puta.*"

Paulie cracked his knuckles. "Wait 'til I get my hands on that guy."

I gritted my teeth. "Oh no, Paulie. This one's mine. When we get to that motel I'm gonna turn Steve Watson every way but loose."

Too late: a killer had already CUT HIM EVERY WAY BUT LOOSE.

Two squads had roped off the entrance to the driveway. We got out of our news van and I flashed my press credentials. NO DICE. The officer on the scene wouldn't let us by. I saw Doug's friend, my connect who allowed Steve to stay at the motel . . . a motel that was often used as a safe house for snitches to cool their heels.

He told them to let us back and we went. Would I have gone if I knew EXACTLY what I would have to look at?

Yeah. And naw.

Yeah, I needed to know what happened. Yeah, I would want to ask questions to get the skinny from the flatfooted, blue-uniformed, bright-buttoned boys. YEAH.

AND NAW, I didn't want to see a man's scalp peeled back like an onion and his upper torso stuck like a fleshy pincushion and his entire body stuffed inside a huge ice-maker.

The blood ran along the melting cubes, careless and neglected like a finished drink on the bar after last call. I looked in at the body. Most of the lower torso was covered in ice. I could see that his throat had been slashed. The deepest cut was on the RIGHT side and then getting less aggressive going to the left which was toward the outside of the icemaker. The killer was most likely left-handed.

Steve fought, but I don't know how much good it did. He had bruises on the one hand that I could see.

Doug's friend was steaming. "We've never lost a guy stashed here. Officially or unofficially. Get me?"

Got him but good. I'd tried to save this man and he lied, lied about what he knew and how much true danger he was in. It had cost him dearly. I just shook my head. The crime boys pulled up and began doing their thing.

Gunner had the camera on his shoulder filming as he asked questions. "How'd he get stuffed in there like that?"

One of the crime scene investigators explained, "He was a small man. Once he was unconscious, even as—excuse the pun—dead weight, back here away from the main road and all the rooms, someone could slip him in easily."

Paulie threw in his thoughts. "Let me guess: he was stabbed to death."

"Right," the crime scene investigator said. "We recovered the knife. It was up under the body. Odd one too . . . old . . ." He held up the bag. The rusty-handled

weapon had an extensive, curved blade that was speckled with blood.

Choke said, "If he didn't get cut to death he would
have died from gangrene. That knife is older than *my
grandpoppie.*"

"Yep, it's pretty old all right. The lab guys will be
able to tell us more about it for sure."

Paulie patted the crime scene investigator on the
back. "Save yourself some time. That's one of the old
knives they used in the slaughterhouses in the Back of
the Yards neighborhood. Processing meat and stuff."

I looked at the knife. "Chance for prints?"

"Slim to none. The ice damaged the handle pretty
bad. But who knows, maybe we'll get lucky and pull a
print off the side of the icemaker. It would take Her-
culean strength to get this door open without a struggle."

"Speaking of which," I said, "that's our next move.
We need to talk to Herc. Finding out that his friend got
murdered just might loosen up that tongue of his.
MAYBE NOW he'll tell us where Mandy is . . . and this
poor guy won't be *iced for nothing.*"

Gunner threw out a question as he knelt to get a
shot of the evidence tech who was dusting for prints.
"But how are we gonna get another crack at Herc?"

The two things I find heaviest to carry are my luggage during my yearly trip to Jamaica AND grudges. One
is inevitable while the other is optional.

I decided NOT TO CARRY a grudge against Wild
Bill Whelk for freezing me out of this story OR for
swearing out a warrant for my arrest. I hoped that
he wouldn't hold a grudge against me for refusing to

set up Brett for the kill AND for escaping out of that window.

I needed Wild Bill to give the okay for me to talk to Herc. Clarice was back at the station keeping tabs on him. Herc was still in police custody being questioned but so far no charges had been filed. A source did tell us that they found a cell phone number registered in Mandy's name and they were tracking down all the latest calls. The last call had been made yesterday but maybe it would lead to some of Mandy's friends or a place she was hiding. Channel 8 checked out the disconnected cell phone number that Steve gave us. It led nowhere.

To my surprise, Wild Bill Whelk agreed to let us talk to Herc. We got the word through Captain Carey, to whom I had thrown a solid back when the Video Cowboys and I tipped him off to where Herc was handcuffed. If it weren't FOR US, *they wouldn't have him in the first place.*

Herc looked like hell and I told him so. "You're tired and you're dirty. You look just god-awful."

I was trying to let him know that I didn't think he could stand it much longer. That he looked broke down. That was my strategy. I wasn't hating because I knew I was half a sight after ripping and running across the city like a madwoman trying to save Zeke and the other folks in that bank. Herc tried to signify.

"Well your name's Raggedy Ann too, lady. Have you looked in the mirror lately?"

"Pretty is in the mirror. Character is in the gut."

Herc sighed and let his tongue roll around against

the insides of his jaws, poking them out like ballooning sails. *That shut his trifling butt up. For real.*

We were in a room very much like the dingy, cramped, dirty one I had been in earlier. Herc was sitting at the table with his right hand cuffed to the table leg. One wall of the room was one-way glass; on the other side I knew that the Video Cowboys and Captain Carey were watching and listening.

"The police say that you haven't been cooperating, Herc."

"Is that right? Maybe because my cooperating mood was pissed on by a crusading journalist and a bunch of broke-down cameramen who fed me nothing but bull. How's about that, huh? SO 'scuse me if I'm TOO FULL to swallow any more garbage from ANY of you guys."

"Herc, I'd be mad if I were you too . . ."

"Cut me some slack, will ya? Don't soft-sell me."

"Look, we would have NEVER come at you like that under normal circumstances. But that bank is FULL of people who are living on hope, the hope that some-body'll find Mandy so that her father will let them go. One of those people means a lot to me so I'm not ashamed to say, *yeah we faked the funk with you.* We were desperate. And guess what?"

Herc just cocked his head and threw me an arrogant glance.

"Mandy's father is getting antsy and desperate too."

Herc looked away.

"You got any kids, Herc?"

"Not that I'm claiming," he smirked.

"You think this is funny? Time to be cute? What makes you think Mandy is safe out there? Huh?"

"She's probably doing better than me."

"There's a pregnant woman and a little boy in that bank. What do ya wanna bet he's scared even though his mommy is with him? Can you put yourself in his shoes, Herc? You were a kid once."

"Barely. I was in and out of foster homes, lady, and that opens your eyes to the slime of the world real quick. NOT GROWING UP isn't an option."

I softened my tone. "Sounds like you had it rough, Herc."

"Rough is right." Herc looked down at the table, his one free hand drawing circles on the metal. "I had to grow up by the time I was eight or nine. I was shuffled around from place to place, afraid to go to sleep 'cause the bigger boys liked to beat us up at night. And when I reached eighteen, being a ward of the state, it was like SEE YA. You're on your own." Herc looked up. "Well I don't care what you say or think. I done good. I done good to keep my mind, my courage, and my wits about me. I DONE GOOD."

"*But you can do better Herc.* You can save those people in there: that little boy who's the same age as you were when you were TOO SCARED to go to sleep at night. Help him to get home and to be able to get a good night's sleep, huh?"

Herc licked his lips before slamming his hand, palm down against the table. He glared at me and I glared back. Then Herc grinned. "You . . . you're good. You almost had me for a minute."

"I'm not playing, Herc. These are real people. Why wouldn't you feel something for them? You're human."

"Right BUT it ain't my problem and it ain't my fault."

"Is it your fault that your friend got murdered today?"

Herc leaned up and his massive chest nearly touched the top of the table. He leaned like he was deaf and needed to close in space to read my lips. His already bloodshot eyes narrowed. A single word escaped his barely parting lips. And that word was, "What?"

This took me by surprise. Not that Herc was some heartless heathen who managed to snake his way above ground ALTHOUGH *he was close*. But the emotion that erupted in his eyes and stretched the skin around his Adam's apple as he swallowed hard seemed too steep for a shallow friendship.

"What happened? Tell me?" His eyes began to tear up. "Huh? What?"

I spoke deliberately. "Steve Watson. He was stabbed to death."

Herc drew a clenched fist to his mouth and bit down on his index finger. Then he used that same fist to pound the table. "But you said he was safe. You said he was in some motel out by the airport, safe."

"That's where the killer found him. Steve told us that he wasn't involved in the drug dealing that you and Mandy had going. Said he knew just minor stuff that spilled out between drinks. That's all. We never knew the real danger he was in. So the police didn't put any high profile protective coverage on him. He held his tongue and it cost him, Herc."

Tears rolled down his face.

"He was cut up bad, Herc. The killer used a long, rusty, mean-looking knife. You know who works like that?"

"Trey Manotti," Herc nodded pitifully. "He's an ANI-MAL and treats everybody else like one."

"Your friend didn't deserve to die like that, Herc."

"Stop saying that!"

"What? I saw. AND I REPEAT. Nobody—and I mean nobody—deserves *to die like that.* And what kind of friend are you—"

"Stop saying he was my *friend!*"

"Why?"

"He wasn't just my friend!! He was my lover."

"Your lover?"

Herc blinked hard, trying to dam up the flood of tears. He didn't even look at me. "Yes, my lover."

Child, you coulda knocked me over with the cotton wad out of an aspirin bottle.

"Yeah." Herc noticed my dropped jaw. "We were lovers, what of it?"

"Nothing," I said from the bottom of my heart. "I leave *the judging to Judy.* Grown folks are allowed to do what makes them happy."

That seemed to soothe him a little bit. "Steve and I met in one of those foster homes I was telling you about. He and I stayed in touch no matter where we got moved, we supported each other . . . protected each other . . ." Herc looked away. "Loved each other."

"But what about Mandy, Herc? You had a thing with her too?"

"No. It was Steve and only him. In the circles that I

had to run in—on the job, on the street, you can't let them know you're gay. I'd have *zip credibility*. Since Mandy rolled with me all the time, everybody just AS-SUMED that she was my girlfriend and that Steve was my buddy."

"She had no problem covering for you like that?"

"Why not, lady? Blood is thicker than water. *Mandy is my sister.*"

I just pulled out a chair, sat down, and looked at him all stupid like, as if to say, Please explain.

Herc said. "It's a long story, lady."

I said, "Then talk fast."

"I wasn't in that foster home by myself. Our mother was a prostitute. Stayed in and out of jail. Mandy and I had different fathers. My father didn't give a shit. But Mandy? My little sister lucked out. Brett would keep Mandy for as long as he could, then his mind would go BONG and the state would yank Mandy out of the house and put her back into foster care. But she loved the ground Brett walked on for trying to keep her, for loving her enough to try." Herc grimaced. "He never gave two cents about me but he does love Mandy."

"And Trey Manotti is after you both. Why?"

"He thinks we stole from him."

"Did you, Herc?"

"In his mind, yes. In our minds, no. Look, do you know what a juvie guard makes? Don't figure. It's a freaking disgrace. I met Trey Manotti while he was in juvie jail. He always had a hustle going. Cigarettes. Weed coming in. But some of the boys wanted harder stuff. I'd passed a few cartons of smokes. Then I looked the other way when the weed came through. *I had to get paid.*"

"And hooked too. The connect was Trey Manotti?"

"He was running it, yeah. His family rep gave him juice you wouldn't believe."

I could see where this was going. "Herc, didn't you see that he was just trying to get you locked in? Once you started with the small stuff, the big stuff had to follow and you couldn't say no."

"It was too late by then. The threats came. Plus I needed the money. Once I knew he was determined to start bringing in junk, I could either CASH IN or get CASHED OUT."

"So how do Steve and Mandy fit in?"

"I told Trey that my girl worked for the airlines and made a couple of runs a month to Mexico and that she could bring back some stuff if he cut us in on the deal."

"That was stupid, Herc."

"Hey, I had no hookups. Besides, Mandy was spazzing about getting money to help her father. She thought he was gonna die in that broke-down mental hospital. It was the only way out that she could see."

"And big brother was more than happy to shed some light on a drug scheme that would get him rich at the same time, huh Herc?"

"Hey, I told her WHAT IT WAS, and what she could make, and Mandy made her own choice."

I could sense something beneath the surface. *The brother doth protest too much.* "Maybe you were *just a little jealous* that Mandy had a better job; a father who cared about her."

"That's crap. I love my sister. She got the breaks I

never did, sure. Did that make her better than me? NO.
But her father, Brett? He always acted like Mandy was
better than me."

"And maybe subconsciously you wanted to prove to
him that Mandy wasn't, by pulling her in. Not meaning
any real harm, Herc, but just to prove a point. Maybe?"

Herc dropped his eyes and shook off the truth.
"Don't lay that on me, lady. Mandy BEGGED me to help.
Mandy wanted in, so she was in. Once she started being
a mule, she dug it. And she moved Brett into a better
hospital. It was going great."

"So how'd it fall apart?"

Herc said something so low that I could barely hear
it. "What, Herc? What'd ya say?"

"Steve," he grumbled out the word.

"What did he do?"

"Steve got hip to what we were doing. He pressed
and pressed me for details. I gave up the info. Steve said
Trey was ripping us off; said our cut was small potatoes
and we should be getting more."

"And HOW did he KNOW THAT?"

"Steve hustled the streets. Ever since we were kids
in the foster home he would scam and steal from folks
on the outside. Then Steve would buy up goodies and
come back home and spread it around. That'd make
everybody like him or at least leave us alone. Steve
thought he could buy people. And most of the time he
was right."

I shrugged. "I don't know, Herc. I can't see him
being that cold and calculating. Steve had a face like one
of the Cosby kids."

"Too bad he didn't get discovered like one of 'em because he sure could act. With that face, Steve could put on a sob story and tell lies and you'd believe every word he said."

"Yeah, speaking of. Steve told us he was married with a couple of kids. He even showed us a picture."

"That was his cousin and her kids. At first she didn't want to have anything to do with Steve, with his father being the black sheep of the family and all. But after he started buying the kids stuff, she'd let him come around during the holidays."

"Okay, Herc, answer me this. How did Steve figure to get more money out of Trey Manotti on your drug deals?"

Herc laughed. "Well, it's not like a boss where we would just go in and ask for a raise. Please. Steve came up with a way for us to siphon off some of the pure junk. He had this guy he knew from the streets who could mix in some powders so the weight would be the same but the goods just weren't as pure. Trey didn't even notice. Steve started selling ours on the street."

"And the money got real good then, huh."

"You know it lady."

"Then where'd it all go, Herc? That place you and Mandy had wasn't *nothin' to write home about*. Didn't see any fancy clothes. That was near 'bout Al Capone's Caddie y'all were driving in. Where's the cash?"

"Hey, Mandy's money went to her dad's hospital bills. And hospitals ain't cheap. Steve and me, we partied. We checked out all the best restaurants, all the best clubs. Steve and me practically lived in Vegas. And that's when things started getting messed up. We started gambling on sports."

"And after a while it wasn't just in Vegas either. You brought the monkey home with you."

"Lady, you're talking like you were there. I got in so deep it makes me sick to the stomach to think about it. The drug money went poof. The job money. I started pulling stickups."

"That's the wanted poster Brett had of you in the bank. The one he held up for the cameras."

"Yeah, but I didn't hurt nobody and I never would have done any of that if I wasn't so deep in trouble. It happened so *fast*. I was desperate, understand?"

"Yeah Herc. So what? You started stepping on the cocaine even more then."

"And Trey still didn't find out until WELL after Steve was out on parole and he was out of juvie."

"What did Steve get busted for?"

"Selling. That's how he got locked up. We'd set up shop outside one of the colleges and it was going pretty smooth until Steve got careless. But remember what I told you about Steve? He always manages to keep some wiggle room. He traded the cops some hot info and got out on parole."

"And he used your and Mandy's address. That was his parole officer who got killed in your apartment."

"Right."

"Was the parole officer in on your drug thing, Herc?"

"Naw. He'd been trying to track Steve down because he found out that he had lied about where he worked. Steve told him that he worked at the shoeshine parlor next door where you found us. But he REALLY was out at the airport. Mandy got Steve a job running the employee shuttle."

"Why?"

"Two reasons. The job had started watching Mandy. They got suspicious. Mandy knew she was being watched so she was too scared to keep bringing the drugs in. Steve thought if he could get a job at the airport that he could convince one of the other flight attendants to start being a mule."

"How'd Mandy get him a job like that in the first place, with the record he had and all?"

"Mandy had a girlfriend in human resources. He dropped his first name, Michael, too, just in case. Faked the soc-number. No one checked."

"And when the parole officer figured it out, he went after Steve?"

"He was in the wrong place at the wrong time. He must have run into Trey. That sick bastard gets his jollies off of hurting people. Saw it in juvie."

"So why not run?"

"Because Steve HAD CONVINCED one of the girls to bring in a load. We were waiting for it to get in, turn it around, and then we'd have enough money to get away from everything."

"So you were waiting to score some drugs. When?"

Herc hesitated.

"Have the drugs come in yet OR NOT?"

"Lady, that's the only bargaining chip I got left. Steve is dead so he can't make the pickup. Mandy DOESN'T EVEN KNOW *the wheres and whens*. And I'm quite sure that the cops aren't gonna let me out of here to go get it myself. I think I'll save something for a little insurance."

"Yeah, but we need Mandy. And we need her NOW to save those people in the bank. And who knows, Herc? Trey just might find her before we do IF you don't help."

"He won't find her. Not in a million years."

"I'll bet that's what Steve thought too."

Herc just dropped his eyes.

"So, the way I see it, Herc, you have two choices you can make—just like the turtle and the hare."

"Meaning what?"

"Meaning you can be a hare and keep running from trouble. OR you can be a turtle and stick your neck out and stop hiding."

As hiding places go, they had *picked a lulu*. Who would have thought to look for Mandy at a drag show theater? Queens Parlor was located on the near west side, which in recent years had begun to boom with upscale condos and nice restaurants, as well as Oprah's Harpo Studios. But Queens Parlor was there when this area was known as Chicago's Skid Row, populated by those who drank too much and cared too little about themselves and their families.

The building was perfect for the fabulous drag shows that they put on night after night every week. It was *over-the-top ornate;* gothic columns would welcome visitors as they approached the entrance. White, gold, and teal paint speckled a series of lion heads that were carved into the stone around the arched double doorway. The lions roared. The rims of their jaws were painted roguish red. Every December 31, the performers would hook their most colorful garters from the teeth: a tradition that was supposed to ensure a prosperous new year.

As the neighborhood limped toward *upscaledom*, the alderman talked about shutting down Queens Parlor. But to HIS SURPRISE the loudest cry of support came from the young up-and-comers who were moving into the area. *They* thought the theater was fun and hip. Herc told us that Mandy was being hidden there by one of Steve's friends who worked at Queens Parlor. His name was Rio.

When we entered the theater we saw a huge photomontage of all the performers. The BIGGEST photo was a head shot of Rio. He was the manager and choreographer of all the performances that featured fabulous drag queens imitating Diana Ross, Barbra Streisand, and retro Broadway shows like *42nd Street* and *Kiss Me Kate*.

At the rear of Queens Parlor was a huge garage with an apartment built over it. In the 1940s the original owner of the place had it custom-made brick by brick, extra wide because he had a fetish for sports cars. Now it stored the props needed for the elaborate shows while doubling as a little cool-out place for the choreographer—BUT TODAY it was a hideaway for MANDY.

We moved in with the police. Captain Carey told his troops to allow us to tag along because we had delivered Herc to them in the first place and I WAS THE ONE who got him to talk.

Our orders were direct. We were to stay behind the lead cops. We could videotape since Mandy didn't have a record and was believed to be unarmed.

The rear of the building was covered. Two officers were there in case Mandy tried to escape on foot. We walked up the apartment's outdoor wooden stairs, obviously tacked on in recent years. As soon as we reached the door, we heard a scream.

The officers glanced at each other and then threw their shoulders against the door. The wooden frame readily gave way, popping off of the metal hinges. Gunner was filming from behind me. Choke and Paulie were in the alley with the other officers videotaping there. When the door flew open, the two officers charged in.

Our mouths collectively dropped.

Trey Manotti was standing over a man half-dressed in a corset, stockings, and high heels. A wig was tossed in the corner. Makeup was smeared all over his cheek. Blood from a knife wound in the man's stomach was pumping out from between his fingers. Even as his face contorted in pain, I recognized Rio, the manager who had promised to hide and take care of Mandy. *Where was she?*

"Drop the knife!"

Trey calmly let the knife fall from his fingers.

"Step back," one officer said as he moved forward, covering Trey with his service revolver. "Raise your hands above your head."

Trey obeyed.

The first officer walked over and went to search him. The other officer began to kneel over Rio, who was trembling on the floor. Then Rio groaned and convulsed so hard that he turned on his side. The other officer glanced down. That split second was a chance for danger to set in.

And Trey took it. He whipped around and threw an elbow against the officer's jaw. He grabbed the gun out of his hand and jerked the cop in front of him like a human shield.

"Make another sound and he gets it in the skull. Drop the gun."

The gun slipped from the officer's hand, clunking against the tile floor.

"You," he nodded at me. "Pick it up. Bring it here."

I gently picked up the gun and walked slowly over to him.

"Easy like," Trey said, "stick it down in my belt. Easy now."

I did as I was told. I tried the soft sell. "C'mon Trey. There's no way out." I was working to get him to give up. "There are cops downstairs too."

He looked concerned but not worried. "Then I guess there's no where to go but UP!"

Trey slapped the cop upside the head with the gun butt, then slung him to the ground where he landed on top of Rio and the other cop. He grabbed a baton off the prop pile and whirled around, shattering the window behind him. He hopped up on the sill, swung his leg out onto the ledge, and disappeared outside!

I ran to the window in time to see him pull himself up toward the roof. I ducked back when I saw the officers running toward the building.

"Stop! Police!"

They fired off two shots, missing.

Once on top of the roof, Trey began to jump from one garage to the next. An additional shot missed his heel. He stopped, fired back. The officers ducked behind a couple of garbage cans. Trey jumped to another garage. The police squeezed off another round of shots.

One bullet hit Trey in the shoulder but momentum propelled him forward. He grabbed the iron rung of a utility pole with his remaining strong arm, swung around, and then dropped. He landed awkwardly but managed to fire two more shots at the police before tearing off in a sprint.

The cops sprung from behind the garbage cans and took off after him.

Some of the employees heard the shooting and came running outside. The cop kneeling over Rio radioed for an ambulance and it arrived quickly. The paramedics frantically worked on Rio and, thankfully, I heard one of them say, "He's got a chance."

But how many more chances would we have? Brett had threatened to blow up the bank at nightfall and it was already dark. EACH and EVERY lead we'd worked on had gotten us close, *but not on the money.* Exhausted and frustrated, we went inside the theater office to regroup. A couple of the employees who huddled together for comfort were visibly shaken by what had just happened. They had a small television set on that was broadcasting Channel 8.

Just as the Video Cowboys and I sat down, a news break updated us on the latest development at the bank.

Pete:
"Good afternoon everyone.
An intense hostage drama has been going on today at Lake Michigan Bank. A lone bank robber has held sev-

eral people at bay with a gun, threatening to detonate a bomb if his daughter Mandy is not brought safely to the scene. Channel 8 reporter Georgia Barnett has been making an effort to help police find her."

Video of Mandy running in the alley with Georgia following. Pic of Mandy and Herc from their apartment.

Georgia tracked down Mandy but the woman narrowly escaped after a dramatic car chase. Police believe Mandy is involved in drug dealing along with this man, once thought her boyfriend, but who WE NOW KNOW is her half brother Herc Quarterman. Our Georgia Barnett made a dramatic plea to the gunman earlier during a newsbreak.

Replay of the newsbreak.

Dissolve from that tape to the new video of the hostages being released while Pete voices over the video live on set.

Pete:
"Just moments ago, Brett answered that plea. He released ALL the hostages EXCEPT Channel 8 cameraman Zeke Rouster. The other hostages—a security guard, an unemployed construction worker, an ad executive, a bank teller, and a pregnant mother and her young son—WERE ALL able to walk out under their own power. The security guard carried with him a videotape that he smuggled to Channel 8, on orders from the gunman. Here is that tape, airing uncut":

Brett:

"I've been talking to the hostages trying to make them understand that I've been forced into this. I think some do understand. Because of that, and what you said, Georgia, I have decided to release all the hostages EX-CEPT your cameraman. I need at LEAST ONE HOSTAGE to keep the cops out looking for my baby and I need him to communicate with these tapes. But do not be fooled. I will blow up this place with us both in it. I've duct-taped the bomb to my chest and handcuffed us together. It's him and me.

I'm dying inside. When I watched that little boy walk out free, I thought of my own child who is still out there. I've tried like any father to keep her safe. I tried to stay calm, thinking of all the times when we were to-gether years ago and happy. I'm praying for that time again. So please ANYBODY and EVERYBODY help me. Please. The deadline is 8:20 p.m."

Dump tape and go back to Pete on set.

That's the latest from here. We will continue to up-date you throughout the day on this breaking story. Thank you and stay tuned.

At least the hostages were out. But Zeke was still in. And time was running out.

"We're not going to find her," I said. Exhausted, I slithered down in the nearest chair.

Gunner said, "C'mon, Georgia. You don't wanna give up now, do you?"

Paulie just growled. "We've looked everywhere. The

cops are looking too. Where could she be? That kid has gotten nothing but grief all her life, barely a happy moment and it just keeps getting worse and worse for her. The poor kid needs some peace."

I shot up in my seat. "That's it."

Gunner prodded. "What's it?"

"If you were out on your own with a brother in jail, a father in trouble, no money, life on the line—where would you go? *You'd go somewhere you felt safe, of course.* Remember what Brett said earlier? That there was one place where he and Mandy were happy and she felt safe."

Choke said, "What'd he say? A boathouse?"

Paulie snapped his fingers twice. "Yeah. Yeah. By some park, Brett said."

Gunner was feeling it too. "Can't be many of those, can there?"

"Not at all," I high-fived the guys. *"Not at all."*

I called Clarice and we both worked the phones, calling the park district and the police marine unit. According to our sources, there was only one boathouse in the area that was near a park. It was located way up the north shoreline near the suburb of Evanston. The boathouse had been ignored and allowed to deteriorate for years. In short, it was abandoned. Boarded up. Both the park and play lot were neglected too. We headed there, speeding down Lake Shore Drive, making great time.

The Video Cowboys and I made our way around the boathouse. It was getting dusky now and we could see a glowing amber ball of light hovering in the corner. It was secluded but luck was on our side. There was only *one way in* and *one way out* of the structure. The storage house faced the crashing waters of Lake Michigan, which was too high up to jump from and NOT crack your skull open unless you were an experienced and fearless diver.

"Let's go get her, guys."

We opened the door and it creaked, sending the sound riveting throughout the rickety structure. I heard a woman gasp from upstairs and then the sound of running, followed by something falling.

"Go! Go! Go!" Paulie chanted and we started running up the stairs.

I shouted, "Mandy. This is Georgia Barnett and my Channel 8 crew. We don't wanna hurt you. We just wanna take you to your dad."

By the time we reached the doorway at the top of the boathouse, the light had been doused and only the faint evening sky shed some muted sunlight in . . . although not enough to truly see. But we could hear crying coming from one of the corners in the room.

"Mandy," I called out again.

We stepped into the middle of the room straining to see. Choke kicked something over, looked, and said, "It's a lamp." He leaned down to pick it up. "I'm going to light it." He moved his hand slowly and threw his voice in the direction of the whimpering. "Please don't be scared, chica. We're not going to hurt you."

Choke lit the lamp and the yellow glow flashed against the glass like a kid's firecracker. The light found enough brilliance to illuminate Mandy. She was sitting in the corner, hugging her knees to her chest. Her eyes were as big as the bottom of teacups. Mandy's teeth chattered. Her hair was damp against her skull and she couldn't stop whimpering. Then she appeared to struggle for words.

"Take your time," I said walking forward, kneeling next to Mandy. I stroked her head. "Swallow and just say it."

Mandy gulped down air. Then said, "Behind you."

It ain't no fun when the rabbit's got the gun.

Trey Manotti was standing there grunting as the air slunk down into his chest and gurgled around, popping back up in an exhale that sounded like someone gargling with a foul-tasting mouthwash. He had gotten hit. He favored his right shoulder, letting it sag. I could see the blood soaking through his shirt. His left hand held a gun that was aimed at the Video Cowboys and me.

"I finally got smart," he said.

"How?" Gunner asked.

Trey Manotti let the sweat roll down from his forehead into the corners of his mouth before answering. "I stopped trying to find her and just followed YOU and let YOU find her for me."

"Yeah," Paulie said, "but NOW you've got MORE than just some tired and scared female to handle. You got the FOUR OF US to deal with as well. *You can't shoot everybody, kid.*"

Trey frowned. "Don't I freaking know you from somewhere?"

"Yeah, from the neighborhood. I probably changed your diapers, kid."

"Yeah? How'd they smell?"

Paulie took a step toward him.

Trey balked. "Don't be stupid old man. All I want is HER. That's it. She and Herc cheated me. And I want my money."

"I don't have any money!" Mandy was whimpering now. "It's all gone and you know it!"

Trey squeezed off a shot that tore into the wooden crossbeam that rested just inches above Mandy's head.

Gunner and Paulie lunged forward, stopped, and slid when Trey aimed from one to the other. "I don't care who dies or how many. So back off, huh?"

Gunner and Paulie froze like little boys playing a kid's game. Trey turned his caustic attention back to Mandy.

"*I'm not surprised you pissed all the money away,* BUT I ALSO KNOW that Steve had a shipment coming in to the airport. I need YOU to get that package for me. That'll more than cover what you guys owe me."

I asked him, "Is that package of coke worth all those lives? The parole officer? Steve? Maybe Rio, the man you hurt at Queens Parlor?"

Trey laughed. "That sympathy stuff belongs on TV, Georgia. I handle my business."

"*You liked it.*"

"Yeah I got off. Not as much as I COULD WITH YOU if we were here alone *but maybe another time, another place.*"

"In your dreams."

"Black bitch."

"BUT NOT your black bitch, huh?"

Trey aimed the gun at me.

Paulie yelled, "Hey punk!"

Gunner lunged. Trey fired. The bullet caught Paulie in the arm. Gunner and Choke were on Trey now, stomping the little punk.

I went over to Mandy and helped her up. She began sobbing into my shoulder. I told her, "Hang on girl. It's almost over."

We called the police and they rushed to the scene to arrest Trey Manotti. He went kicking and screaming like the tantrum-loving brat that he was. MAYBE when he got locked up THIS TIME, some of the men would teach him some manners.

An ambulance came for Paulie too. *That nut had the nerve to say,* "Hey, if that punk Trey can walk around with a slug in him SO CAN I. Let me go with you, guys."

Choke said something in Spanish.

I said what I hoped he said, "Not on your life boy. You're hurt. Besides, we couldn't make it back in time to meet Brett's deadline even with your Indy 500 driving."

"So now what?" Paulie asked.

I had a plan. I called Clarice and told her that we were going to go live and let Brett know that we had Mandy safe and sound. Maybe if Brett saw her on TV, he would give us the extra time we needed to get Mandy to the bank.

But my motto for the day should have been, *Got a plan? Got a problem,* 'cause that's when our old faithful truck conked completely out. We couldn't get the antenna up. It was stuck. AND SO WERE WE.

Choke was swearing something fierce. Mandy was crying and I was near tears myself. Gunner was trying to work on it.

I got on my cell and called Captain Carey. He had given me his number and right about now was the best time to use it.

"Hello. Carey," he said.

"Captain. This is Georgia Barnett. I gotta talk to Bill. Put him on, please. I've got Mandy."

"You got her?" he repeated.

Wild Bill snatched the phone. "Georgia? You've got her?"

"Yes! Yes! We got her but we're out near Evanston along the lakeshore. We can't drive in fast enough to meet Brett's deadline. And we had an equipment failure and I can't go live and put Mandy on TV to show Brett that she's really safe. So you gotta get the phone company to patch this call into the bank so Mandy can talk to him."

"Too late, Georgia."

"Whatdaya mean it's too late, Bill?"

"I mean we have to take action NOW. Brett is so far off his rocker he probably wouldn't even take the call, let alone believe it. You can't get here so we're going with plan B." The phone line went CLICK!

"Wait! Wait!"

I called back again. Captain Carey got back on the line. "Sorry, Georgia."

"Wait, what's plan B? Can you just tell me that?"

"Snipers." Then he hung up.

Oh God.

"What?" Mandy asked urgently. "What's going on? Are they gonna hurt my father?"

"NOT if we can get you there in time, Mandy." I started to pace. "But how can we get you there in time? *We'd need wings.*"

The ambulance driver who was helping Paulie into the back of the vehicle said, "I know where you can get some wings."

And it wasn't from heaven.

We wound up on the rooftop of a hospital in Evanston that was only four blocks away. They had a heliport there for emergencies. Choppers would land and take off with critical patients. And right about now NOTHING was *more critical* than the situation we were in.

Gunner took one look at the chopper and grinned, "Who wants to take a spin with an old soldier like me?"

So Gunner, Mandy, Choke, and I got in. I called Clarice to make sure we stayed hot with our live crew on the ground. If Wild Bill did something stupid, I wanted there to be PLENTY of evidence of it later. I told her to have Pete announce that we had Mandy and were coming in. Then I told her that we had commandeered a chopper and to expect an angry call from the hospital.

"Who's flying it?"

"Gunner."

"Well if anybody can do it, he can," Clarice said. "Still, be careful. When was the last time Gunner flew a chopper?"

I yelled over the whirling propellers. "Clarice asked when was the last time you flew a chopper?"

"What?"

"I SAID WHEN WAS THE LAST TIME YOU FLEW A CHOPPER?"

He thought before grabbing the throttle. "When Johnson was in office."

Then up we went.

"What did he say?" Clarice asked. "I can't hear, Georgia."

I didn't EVEN WANNA repeat it. It was scary enough just hearing about it. And Choke was sitting there holding the little cross he wore around his neck, praying in Spanish.

Gunner laughed, "Is he really THAT nervous?"

The whirling sound of the chopper cut through the air. Mandy bit down on her bottom lip as she watched the blue Lake Michigan waters curl and cuddle against the shoreline. A mischievous wind occasionally teased us, pitching the chopper to the left, then to the right.

My heart was pounding and my stomach was a bit on the queasy side as the chopper began to bounce when our momentum surged. I was so glad that I had NOT eaten anything heavy 'cause it *sure would have come up in a hurry.*

We only had one place to land that would allow us to get to the bank in time to save Brett and Zeke. That place was the top of the Hilton hotel downtown on Michigan Avenue. There was a landing pad there from way back when the hotel was a favorite staying place of visiting presidents and foreign heads of state.

Channel 8 had told them the deal and we'd been

cleared to land there. I called my girl Sylvia at her cop shop. She was sending a police escort to wait for us on the street to drive us over to the bank only a mile away.

The whirling sound of the propellers had beat down my poor eardrums. Because of the temporary hearing loss, everything my eyes engaged grew to gigantic proportions. The clouds looked bigger. The waves rolled higher. The landing pad seemed massive.

Gunner brought the chopper lower and lower, rocking it gently back and forth before touching its metal feet down. I opened the door and began to get out. Me first. Then Mandy. Finally Choke.

"We don't have much time!" I yelled at Gunner, who for some reason had not killed the motor. "C'mon."

Gunner shook his head no before saying, "I gotta get this back. Suppose the hospital needs it?"

Then we stepped back and Gunner began to take off again. *Oh Lord, I was down to only one Video Cowboy.*

The three of us ran for the door and got downstairs as fast as we could. The police cars were there, waiting, motors running. We jumped inside. The screeching sirens parted the waves of traffic. On the radio, an announcer was giving a live update.

Sources tell us that the gunman's daughter has been found but may not make it to the bank in time. As the deadline quickly approaches, police officers here at the scene are expressing grave concern that the gunman will make good on his threat to blow up the bank. Just moments ago, officers made members of the media back off the police barrier that was already well away from the bank. We'll update you with more information as it becomes available.

My cell phone rang.

The cars in front of us were slow to get out of the way. We slammed on the brakes and swerved around a cab.

It was Clarice on the line. "Hey girl. The cops grounded all news choppers BUT before they landed, the crew said that they could see the snipers moving into place."

The squad car lurched forward again, stopped, and then continued weaving through the heavy traffic. The cop who was driving cussed, "Get outta the way! Get outta the way!"

Clarice's voice sounded heavy and sad. "It's getting scary, girl."

"You're right, Clarice. But it just doesn't make sense. I don't care how sharp the shooters are, the only clear line of fire would be to lure Brett to the door."

Mandy said, "Daddy won't go to the door. Not unless he sees me."

That's when it hit me.

"Oh God! Clarice?"

"Yeah girl."

"When did Pete go live and announce that we had Mandy and were on our way?"

"Like a minute ago when you told us to. He's about to hit air again. You want me to put the phone up to the monitor so you can listen?"

"No. Think about this. We were the ONLY ones who

knew that we got Mandy, Clarice. But I just heard a cut they've been running on one of the radio stations. How'd they get that on air BEFORE US?"

"An inside source, maybe? Or someone at the hospital called the radio station."

"Naw, Clarice, they wouldn't go with the story UNLESS they confirmed it with the police TOO and there wasn't enough time for that."

"So whataya saying, Georgia?"

"The police leaked it earlier before it EVEN happened."

"Why would they do that?"

"It's a trick, Clarice! Brett won't come to that door unless he sees Mandy. OR someone who looks like her. The cops are going to run a decoy at him."

"Oh no," Clarice said. "He'll have heard on our air that she's coming and he'll think it's REALLY her . . ."

"Then get to the door and the snipers . . ."

I yelled at the cop driving, "How soon?"

"Two more blocks, then you're gonna have to get out and run."

Clarice yelled in my ear, "They're making the move, Georgia!"

"What?"

"The ground reporter at the scene says he's hearing that Mandy is there, and being escorted to the front door of the bank."

"She's with me!"

Mandy shouted, "I'm here! I'm here!"

The squad car swerved up through a construction site. "Shortcut," my driver said. "Around this corner, here. Get out and run as soon as I stop."

We just missed the side of a steel beam as the wheels spun and screeched, throwing off sand and gravel. The car lurched to a stop and we jumped out and started running.

Clarice was talking me through it. "They're walking the girl up. We're live from a low-angle lens. We're so far back we can't see the woman's face but the hair and the height look right. She's walking slowly toward the door."

We were running. And running.

"Brett's near the door. I can see Zeke's hand, Georgia. They're still cuffed together."

All of a sudden I hear this consuming noise overhead. It was a booming, whirling sound. I looked up. It's a chopper.

"Clarice, I thought you said the cops grounded all the TV choppers?"

"They did."

I looked again. *It was Gunner.*

That boy did a loop and buzzed down over the cop cars. And I could see all the officers duck. The media that had been backed up ducked as well before pointing upward.

"Brett just stepped back!" Clarice shouted. "Thank God he stepped back."

As we ran closer we could see the fake Mandy hunkered down, the cops distracted by the chopper.

"Who the hell is that in the chopper?" Clarice asked.

"That's a Video Cowboy, baby." I killed my cell as we fought our way forward.

Gunner was buzzing the street, looping.

We pushed and shoved our way to the front of the

media barricade. I bellowed, "That woman is a decoy. It's a trick! This is the REAL MANDY with me."

My colleagues parted when they realized what the heck was going on. A wave of hands hit our backs and pushed us forward; the energetic surge propelled us forward.

Then the COPS STOPPED us cold.

"No media!"

Choke, who had been quiet as a mouse up until this point, barreled forward and threw a shoulder against the two cops, blocking them out like a power forward. "¡Apúrate! ¡Apúrate!" he yelled.

We pushed and squeezed through a tiny sliver of space. I was holding Mandy's hand now, pulling and fighting people away with my free hand. The wind from the chopper whipped up dust and debris from the street and my eyes began to tear.

The fake Mandy was still on the ground covering her head.

I heard a couple of cops shout, "Stop! Stop!"

But we kept on. Kept on. Mandy pushed forward, yelling, "Daddy! Daddy!"

The door of the bank opened and Brett came out, gun pressed up against Zeke's side, their hands handcuffed together. When he saw her, his eyes lit up and his gun hand dropped as he opened that arm to let her sail into his embrace.

That's when I heard the shot. Not from one of the snipers held at bay by Gunner in the chopper, but from the ground. It was a terrible, horrible sound.

I slumped to the ground and buried my head in my hands.

The shot hit Brett in the chest. A puff of red sprayed from the wound as his body weight anchored him toward the ground. Brett dropped, pulling Zeke down with him, as they remained handcuffed together.

Mandy hovered over her father, screaming. I got up and ran to Zeke. His eyes were blinking rapid-fire as if he were struggling to regain stolen sight. His clothes were moist with sweat, the rims of his eyebrows dotted with perspiration. Zeke said TWICE before I could even ask ONCE, "I'm okay. I'm okay."

Then I heard Brett pant, "The bomb is activated . . ."

When he fell, the impact with the ground set off the timer.

Two cops over my shoulders yelled, "Bomb squad! Everybody else get back! Get back!" They grabbed Mandy and me and began pulling us away.

Brett whizzed, "No time . . . less than a minute now." He pointed at his pocket and looked at me. "Box cutter."

I broke free from the cop and knelt on the ground. I grabbed the metal-handled tool with the razor blade edge. My hands were trembling. "Now what?"

"Two wires."

"I see. What? What?"

"Red and yellow." Brett's eyes rolled up in the back of his head. "Cut the . . ."

Cut the what?

Then Brett passed out. His shirt was completely soaked in blood. I glanced all around; the people spun in my sight. I heard yelling.

"Get outta there!"

Zeke panted, "Cut one."

"Which one?"

"Time's running out!"

Red or yellow. Yellow or red.

I swallowed, and said, "God, you know." Then I cut one.

I love me some red.

Red is the color of: my sorority, my favorite flower, my favorite fruit, and the sandy bottom in the river that runs through my great-grandparents' home in the Deep South.

But to the world at large, RED, they say, means danger. *Stop. Hold up. Warning . . . warning Will Robinson and the like.* But here's where I'm coming from: KNOWING that Brett was unstable when he constructed the bomb PLUS the fact that red has always been a lucky color for me—my gut said red is good SO I cut the yellow.

Good thing too.

'Cause altogether, I'm fine. But I don't think I'd be nary too cute blown up into bits and pieces.

Do you?

After my ordeal, I called my mother and my man. Doug's voice cracked with emotion. "Girl, you do believe in running the table, don't you? You're a lucky lady and I'm lucky to have you. I can't wait to get home and hold you, G."

And I couldn't hold back my emotions any longer. I wept quietly.

When I gathered myself after killing a box of Puffs, I went to the hospital to see my man Zeke. They had decided to keep him overnight for observation.

"Nice job, Georgia." Zeke was half-grinning but his voice quivered and his eyes were moist. "You saved my butt. C'mere."

I went to his bedside and we hugged. "Go 'head. Have a good cry, Zeke. I already had one myself." Seconds later I felt one of his tears against my cheek.

Story Slug = Hostage Standoff
11:00 P.M. Special Report

Pete:

"We interrupt our regular broadcast for this report: the latest developments in a dramatic hostage situation at Lake Michigan Bank. It all started when Brett Andronte walked into the bank with a gun and a bomb, took hostages, and demanded that his wayward daughter Mandy be brought to him OR ELSE.

Events then began to unfold . . . murders, drug dealing, mob connections, and the like. Joining us now for a recap of the day's dramatic events is Channel 8's Georgia Barnett, who at one time was a hostage herself.

Georgia?"

Georgia:

"Thank you Pete.

This morning, my cameraman Zeke Rouster and I found ourselves being held hostage inside Lake Michigan Bank. I was let go to help find Brett Andronte's daughter. I filed numerous reports . . . communicating back and forth with him via videotape and newsbreaks. It's a day that I will never forget."

Take the videotaped package with my voice recapping events.

The first video shows a photo of Herc, Mandy, and Steve in New Orleans that was found in the lockbox.

The people in this picture cherish the photograph. But tonight because of a drug dealing scheme gone wrong . . . one of them is dead and the other two are behind bars.

Take photo of Trey Manotti mug shot.

All three of them were on the run from this man: Trey Manotti, a young, violent drug dealer from a well-known Chicago crime family.

Shot of planes taking off at Midway. Then exterior of juvie jail.

Police say Mandy smuggled in drugs from Mexico while working as a flight attendant for Red Eye Airlines. She was put in contact with Manotti by her half brother Herc Quarterman, who met the young mobster while working at a juvenile jail.

Cut to photo of Mandy and her dad Brett. Then mug shot of Michael Steven Watson. File shot of cocaine.

Mandy told police that she entered the drug business to get money to help her mentally ill father, Brett. But things went terribly wrong when her brother's lover got into the picture. Michael S. Watson, also known as

Steve, had a long rap sheet of petty street crimes. He wanted in on the cocaine deal. His desire to get in, and his desire to cut Manotti out, cost him his life.

Cut to body bag, icemaker, and knife at the motel where Steve was killed. Plus cop cars.

Steve's body was found stuffed in this icemaker at a hotel out by Midway Airport. Police say the fingerprints on the icemaker match those of Trey Manotti. Steve was waiting for a cocaine delivery to come in so that he, Herc, and Mandy could get away. But Trey Manotti allegedly found him first. Next he wanted Mandy.

Cut to work ID of Mandy, then the veterans' hospital.

But Mandy did not want to abandon her father, who had left the mental hospital where he had been staying to search for his daughter once she and Herc first went into hiding several days ago. After a visit to the hospital last week, he had sensed that Mandy was in danger.

Dissolve to B-roll of video that Zeke took of Brett inside the bank, holding up the police alert of Herc. Then change to B-roll of Brett pacing back and forth.

That danger involved the man on this police alert: Herc Quarterman. Angry, disoriented, and refusing to take his medication, Brett decided to take drastic measures when the police and his doctors wouldn't look for his daughter—by forcing his way into the bank and taking hostages.

Cut to video of me chasing Mandy. Walking shot of Herc being arrested. Exterior of Queens Parlor.

I was released to try and find Mandy. I came close to catching her here but she escaped after crashing her car into the side of a building. Her brother Herc was arrested and told us that Mandy was hiding out with a friend named Rio who manages the infamous drag theater known as Queens Parlor.

B-roll of cops kicking in the door. Next shot: Trey with a knife. Shot of Rio on floor, bleeding, pan back to Trey.

Trey Manotti, of the infamous Manotti clan, had been stalking Mandy, who was a partner in the drug scheme. Like us, he went looking for Mandy at the famous west side drag theater. There police caught him standing over the manager Rio, who had been beaten and stabbed.

Video of Trey getting the cop's gun, and jumping out the window.

Just minutes before this attempt to arrest Manotti—as you watch your screen—you'll see him get the officer's gun. Afterward, the camera falls to the floor.

Trey escaped out of the window but not before police shot him in the arm.

B-roll of hostages being released. Cut to shot of videotape with Brett handcuffed to Zeke.

After a frantic plea from me, Brett released all of the remaining hostages EXCEPT for Channel 8 cameraman Zeke Rouster. Brett handcuffed himself to Zeke and forced the cameraman to use duct tape to secure the bomb to his stomach.

B-roll of the north shore boathouse.

We tracked Mandy down to this boathouse, now abandoned, but once a favorite of Mandy and her father when she was a little girl.

Next a shot of Mandy on the floor, trembling. Cut to Trey being arrested and put in a cop car.

We found her inside. Little did we know that Trey Manotti had followed us. But through the quick action of my video crew, they were able to capture Trey and have him arrested for murder and various other charges.

Cop car pulling away with Trey inside. Mandy cries.

With Trey in cuffs, our next move was to get Mandy to her father by sundown to keep him from carrying out his threat to blow up the bank.
The Channel 8 crew borrowed a chopper from a nearby hospital, landing on top of the Hilton on Michigan Avenue. With a police escort we got as close as we could, then sprinted toward the bank.

B-roll of fake Mandy outside of bank. B-roll of Gunner in chopper, buzzing crowd.

A policewoman pretending to be Mandy was being used as a decoy to lure Brett outside for a sniper shot. But quick action by a freelance cameraman kept the snipers at bay as the chopper buzzed the crowd until Mandy and I were able to get to the scene.

B-roll of Brett coming out to Mandy, opening his arms, getting shot.

Brett ran outside with his remaining hostage cuffed to his wrist and the bomb taped to his chest. Just seconds before he tried to hug his daughter, a cop on the ground shot him.

Video of me with box cutters. Cutting wires on the bomb taped to his chest.

Brett's fall activated the homemade bomb. Before he passed out from loss of blood, Brett told me to cut a wire to disarm the explosive. Thank God I picked the right one.

Chicago police were able to intercept the cocaine shipment that Mandy, Herc, and Steve had been waiting for—that Trey Manotti had killed for. A flight attendant is behind bars tonight charged with drug trafficking.

Dump tape, come back to set to Georgia for live tag on camera.

Meanwhile tonight, Brett Andronte remains hospitalized in good condition with a chest wound. Authorities say he will fully recover. His daughter Mandy is in police custody and has agreed to testify against Trey Manotti in exchange for a reduced sentence for her brother and father, as well as relocation in the witness protection program. The bike messenger shot inside the bank during the hostage siege is expected to fully recover as well.

Cameraman Zeke Rouster, who was also held hostage, and who bravely shot the video, is being hospitalized overnight because of this harrowing ordeal. We all owe a debt of thanks to a group of feisty freelance cameramen nicknamed the Video Cowboys: Vicente "Choke" Ochoa, Paulie Vitale, and Wayne "Gunner" Anderson, who, incidentally, are already fielding offers from local news stations.

As for this reporter, it's been a long day and an even longer night. I'm happy to know the Video Cowboys, and happier still that everyone got out of that bank alive. I'm Georgia Barnett, Channel 8 News.

YOLANDA JOE is the Blackboard best-selling author of *Details at Ten; This Just In . . .; Bebe's By Golly Wow; He Say, She Say;* and *Falling Leaves of Ivy.* She is a freelance journalist who has written for CBS, WGN, the *Chicago Tribune, The New York Times,* and *The Washington Post.* Joe teaches writing at the City Colleges of Chicago. She is a graduate of Yale University and Columbia University School of Journalism.

Mystery JOE
Joe, Yolanda.
Video cowboys : a Georgia
  Barnett mystery